# LEFT BEHIND

## >THE KIDS<

# Jerry B. Jenkins

# Tim LaHaye

### WITH CHRIS FABRY

TYNDALE HOUSE PUBLISHERS, INC.
WHEATON, ILLINOIS

Visit Tyndale's exciting Web site at www.tyndale.com

Discover the latest Left Behind news at www.leftbehind.com

Published in association with the literary agency of Alive Communications, Inc., 7680 Goddard Street, Suite 200, Colorado Springs, CO 80920.

Edited by Lorie Popp

ISBN 0-8423-5802-1, mass paper

Printed in the United States of America

08  07  06  05  04  03
8   7   6   5   4   3   2   1

To the Padrnos Family:
Nicholas, Daniel, Benjamin, Jonathan,
Carla, and Coach Tom

# TABLE OF CONTENTS

**About the Authors**

## THE YOUNG TRIBULATION FORCE

**Original members**—Vicki Byrne, Judd Thompson, Lionel Washington

**Other members**—Mark, Conrad, Darrion, Janie, Charlie, Shelly, Melinda

## OTHER BELIEVERS

**Jim Dekker**—GC satellite operator helping the kids

**Chang Wong**—Chinese teenager working in New Babylon

**Cheryl Tifanne**—pregnant young lady from Iowa

**Westin Jakes**—pilot for singer Z-Van

**Tsion Ben-Judah**—Jewish scholar who writes about prophecy

**Colin and Becky Dial**—Wisconsin couple with an underground hideout

**Bo and Ginny Shairton and Maggie Carlson**—escapees from GC jail

**Sam Goldberg**—Jewish teenager, Lionel's good friend

**Mr. Mitchell Stein**—Jewish friend of the Young Trib Force

**Chaim Rosenzweig**—famous Israeli scientist

**Thomas and Josey Fogarty**—former policeman/Peacekeeper and his wife

## UNBELIEVERS

**Nicolae Carpathia**—leader of the Global Community

**Leon Fortunato**—Carpathia's right-hand man

**Z-Van**—lead singer for the popular group, The Four Horsemen

## UNDECIDED

**Anita Aguilara**—Manny's sister

# What's Gone On Before

JUDD Thompson Jr. and the rest of the Young Tribulation Force are living the adventure of a lifetime. In Jerusalem, Nicolae Carpathia concludes his horrific display of blasphemy and leaves the area. Judd and Lionel follow many unbelievers toward the ancient fort of Masada.

After a harrowing chase, Vicki Byrne and her friends Mark and Manny pull into a gang hideout. Manny stays to tell his sister and fellow gang members what has happened to him, and Vicki and Mark rush to help a GC Morale Monitor. Vicki and Mark barely escape a Global Community plot and are welcomed back to the crowded Wisconsin hideout.

Judd hears updates about the rescue attempt of Jewish believers and unbelievers from his friend Chang Wong in New Babylon. After Judd speaks with Vicki by phone, Dr. Chaim Rosenzweig, now known as

Micah, gives an impassioned speech at Masada. Afterward, Sam Goldberg and Mr. Stein head to Petra as Judd and Lionel race toward Jerusalem. On their way back, GC choppers fall from the sky, a miraculous intervention by God. Westin Jakes, pilot for singer Z-Van, offers to fly Judd and Lionel home, but when they reach the airport the next morning, Z-Van's plane has been destroyed.

Vicki and the others in Wisconsin watch reports about a new plague of blood on the seas. Vicki is alone when an alarm rings inside the hideout. Something moves on the monitor, and Vicki gasps as a strange face fills the screen.

Join the Young Tribulation Force as they struggle to survive the most frightening period in the history of the world and reach out to others with the truth.

# ONE

# The Face

VICKI Byrne gasped, sucking in air, trying to slow her racing heart. She pulled herself up and stood in front of the computer monitor. Whoever was out there had disabled the camera.

A thousand thoughts rushed through her mind. Vicki's first fear was the Global Community. Could they have found the hideout and surrounded Colin's home?

*Slow down*, Vicki thought. The person wasn't wearing a GC uniform, and the hair seemed long and stringy. *Maybe someone's out for a walk in the woods.* No, they were definitely sneaking up on the hideout.

She clicked on another camera and checked the area, but there was no movement.

Vicki put a hand to her forehead and closed her eyes. Maybe her mind was playing tricks. She had heard of that happening to people who were exhausted. Maybe she only thought she saw a face on the camera. She clicked the first camera, and the screen remained blank. There had been someone out there—but who?

Vicki didn't want to wake anyone, especially the guys. She didn't want to be a scared little girl who needed help from the big strong boys. Shelly was the obvious choice to awaken, but Vicki decided against it. What was it? Pride? Fear? She didn't know. All Vicki knew was that there was someone walking around outside Colin Dial's house and she had to find out who it was.

She switched to another camera again and focused on the area where the mystery person could be. Nothing. Not a chipmunk, squirrel, opossum, or scary face in sight.

Vicki shuddered. What if the person was hurt or in some kind of trouble, running from something or someone? She kept looking, trying hard not to ignore her feelings.

Each motion sensor came up empty. Whoever it was had either moved out of the area or was in hiding.

Vicki hesitated before she crept past the room where Shelly and Janie slept and grabbed a wool jacket from the closet. Colin Dial's wife, Becky, had told the group that they could share everything they found in the basement. "You kids need something, use it," she had said.

*Kids.* Vicki smiled at the word. It had been a long time since she felt like a kid. True, she was only seventeen. In a normal world she would have been enjoying her senior year of high school. But this was not a normal world. Each day brought a new set of dangers and problems. She and the others had done their best to think clearly, then react. But there were some things you couldn't plan for, things that went beyond imagination. Like tonight—helicopters falling from the sky, the threat of an all-out war coming from the most evil man in the world.

No, Vicki didn't feel like a kid. She should have been thinking about her senior picture or buying her first car or what she would wear to the prom. For a split second, as she put on the jacket, Vicki let her mind go. She imagined wearing a beautiful dress and walking into Nicolae High, arm in arm with Judd, her red hair flowing over her shoulders.

A motion sensor beeped and snapped her back to reality. She quickly turned it off and glanced at the monitor. A second camera had gone blank.

Something scratched at the other side of

the hideout. Vicki opened a door quietly, and Phoenix scampered up to her, wagging his tail.

"Want to help me?" Vicki whispered.

Phoenix snorted and Vicki led him up the stairs. Going outside was risky, but she had to see who was out there.

Judd stared at the burning wreckage of Z-Van's plane. "I thought we were going home," he muttered.

Lionel put a hand on Judd's shoulder. "I know what you mean. I was looking forward to seeing everybody."

Judd glanced at Westin Jakes, Z-Van's pilot, who spoke to one of the emergency workers near the charred building. Westin pulled out his cell phone as he walked toward Judd and Lionel. "A GC chopper tried an emergency landing late last night but didn't make it."

"What do we do now?" Judd said.

"Make other plans. Z-Van can get another plane as fast as he wants. Maybe a day or two."

"Can we fly commercial?" Lionel said.

"Planes have been grounded because of the activity last night," Westin said. "Plus, I hear they're requiring people to have the mark to make it through security."

Judd ran a hand through his hair. "We can't go back to Z-Van. He'll turn us in."

"Stick with me," Westin said. "I'll call him and explain about the plane. You can stay in my room at the hotel until we figure out a way to get back."

Westin hailed a cab and phoned Z-Van. After he hung up, he told Judd and Lionel that Z-Van had said he should have stayed with the plane.

"Which means you'd be dead," Lionel said.

Westin asked the driver to turn up the radio. A live broadcast had begun, celebrating the lifting of the plague of boils. Crowds screamed and chanted in the background as the announcer ran down the list of participants. When he mentioned Z-Van's name, the crowd went wild.

Westin pecked the driver's back. "Take us to the concert."

Vicki looked for a pair of Colin's night glasses but couldn't find them. She leashed Phoenix and crept outside. She knew the dog would probably bark if he saw something, but she felt safe with him close, even if it did alert the intruder.

She stood by the house and listened,

letting her eyes get accustomed to the moonlight. Finally, she pulled Phoenix's leash tight and set out.

When she reached the tree line, the dog bristled and Vicki stopped. She thought the camera was straight ahead, about another fifty yards, but was it closer?

"It's okay, boy," Vicki whispered, reaching down and putting a hand on the dog's head.

She knelt beside him, her senses heightened. Suddenly she didn't think coming outside had been such a good idea. What if it was the Global Community? What if Claudia Zander had followed her and burst through the woods with a weapon drawn?

As Vicki stood, a twig snapped nearby and Phoenix growled. He shot toward the noise, the leash slipping through Vicki's hands. "No! Come back!"

Phoenix disappeared into the woods. Suddenly there was movement—someone running. Two people, maybe three.

"Here he comes!" a female shouted.

"Go, go, go!" came the reply.

Vicki's heart raced. She followed the barking and footsteps, dodging trees and brush. Her jacket got caught, and she stopped to pull loose from briers.

Phoenix yelped and Vicki screamed, "Don't hurt him!"

Instinct took over as Vicki plunged farther into the woods. She didn't care how many people were out there or if they had guns— they weren't going to hurt Phoenix.

Voices and footsteps melted into the woods. Vicki followed Phoenix's bark until she found him by a pine tree. He was standing on his back legs, the leash tied to one of the lowest branches.

She quickly untied it, clamped her hand around his mouth, and listened. Night sounds. Soft chirping of crickets. A small animal skittered across a downed tree in front of her. After a few moments, she decided whoever had been out here was gone. She wrapped the leash around her hand and headed back to the house.

On her way she spotted the soft, red glow of a light on a tree, head high. The tiny camera had been covered with a cloth about the size of a handkerchief. Vicki uncovered the camera and moved to her right, where she knew the second camera had gone blank. This time she found a small glove placed over a lens at the base of a tree.

She stuffed the cloth and glove in her jacket and returned to the house. Inside, Vicki put Phoenix downstairs and turned on the kitchen light to inspect the items. One turned out to be a child's glove, with black, orange, and yellow rings around the fingers. The sight immediately made her think of her little sister, Jeanni. How many times had Vicki helped Jeanni put on gloves so she could play in the snow?

She looked inside the glove for a tag or anything to identify where it had come from, but there was nothing. The piece of cloth was indeed a handkerchief with a series of red rectangles. On the bottom-right corner, Vicki noticed someone had crudely embroidered the letters *MM* with dark thread.

She turned off the lights and took the items downstairs to the hideout. Vicki knew the others would be upset with her, but she had resigned herself to waking them.

As she passed the main computer, she glanced at the screen and gasped. Something had been placed in front of one of the cameras. Vicki enlarged the view and read two words, scrawled in crayon on a scrap of white paper propped in front of the camera:

*Help me.*

Judd called Chang Wong's number and left a message as he headed toward the celebration with Westin and Lionel. Westin didn't explain why they were going, and Judd admitted a certain curiosity at what Z-Van had planned.

Chang called back a few minutes later and told Judd he was at work in a secure location. Operation Eagle had gone well, though the man Chang had taken over for in New Babylon, David Hassid, had been killed by GC forces near Petra.

"Last night was incredible," Chang said. "Not one Tribulation Force aircraft was lost, but hundreds of Global Community people died."

Judd explained where they were headed and Chang groaned. "Only Nicolae would celebrate after such a defeat. I've been assigned by my supervisor to monitor deaths of people due to the BIO disaster."

"BIO?"

"Blood In Ocean," Chang said. "The lakes and rivers haven't been affected."

"I wish we could talk with Dr. Ben-Judah about that and find out why," Judd said. "You mentioned that they suspect a mole inside New Babylon. Are you still in danger?"

"I think I'm okay. I work in an office with about thirty others. I'm trying not to say much to anyone. My superior, Mr. Figueroa, told me this morning that Supreme Commander Moon had been killed."

"You already knew that," Judd said.

"Yes, but he said they suspect two airplane stewards of committing the crime. He thinks they are the ones with the contact on the inside."

"That's insane!" Judd said. "You told me yourself that you heard Carpathia kill Moon. There were other people in the room."

"Lying is normal around here," Chang said. "I'd better get back. I'll call you later to hear about the celebration."

The cab pulled up to the massive outdoor venue just as Dr. Neal Damosa, the Global Community's top education guru, took the stage. "From Jerusalem to Bangladesh, from London to Marrakesh, from Tokyo to Sydney, we welcome the world to this celebration!"

The crowd, pushed into the makeshift arena, clapped politely as Damosa welcomed honored guests. "But some of the most treasured participants of this gathering are right here in front of the crowd." He motioned, and the camera quickly panned the front row of spectators. Judd felt his stomach turn when he looked at the massive video display above the stage. The camera caught at least a hundred young people who had taken Carpathia's mark.

"These and many of you around the world are now part of the new society being raised up by our potentate and our god, Nicolae Carpathia!"

The huge screen over the stage switched to different locations around the world. Young and old alike went wild at the mention of Nicolae's name. Evidently they thought the man would make an appearance at the gathering. Instead, Damosa urged those who hadn't yet taken the mark to do it that day in the new loyalty mark centers just opened.

Judd noticed filmmaker Lars Rahlmost at the front of the stage, directing his camera operator and talking into a handheld radio.

"And now, the moment we've all been waiting for," Damosa crooned, putting on dark sunglasses that brought new cheers from the crowd. "Here to debut songs from his new project, *Resurrection*, is the first civilian to take the mark of loyalty, Z-Van—and The Four Horsemen!"

Sam Goldberg had lived through the most thrilling night of his life. After they left Masada, the drive through the desert to Petra had been filled with twists and turns. Chased by the Global Community, their truck had actually been stopped by Peacekeepers, but the band of new believers kept going. At one point, the earth had opened and swallowed several Global Community vehicles chasing Operation Eagle.

Sam tried to reach Judd via cell phone but couldn't get through. He wanted to tell Judd about his adventure and the beauty of Petra. But how could he describe it? He had been there as a youngster with his family, walking through the Siq, a narrow, mile-long walkway. But he hadn't appreciated the city carved out of rock like he did today. Sam believed this was God's place of protection.

As Operation Eagle leaders guided many to the Siq, Sam stayed behind, looking for his friend Mr. Stein and listening to the conversation of those in charge of Operation Eagle.

Sam scanned the crowd and was glad no one with the mark of Carpathia would enter Petra. But he was distressed when he saw groups of people without God's mark on their foreheads. Would these become believers? Would these betray the company of Christ followers?

Older people shuffled along the entrance. Tiny children slept on parents' shoulders, exhausted from the hurried escape from Nicolae Carpathia and his troops. Though tired, most people seemed excited about what was ahead. Sam heard some talk about Micah, while others said they couldn't wait to hear from Dr. Tsion Ben-Judah, who had promised to fly to Petra and meet with the pilgrims.

Sam started to dial Judd again but hung up before it rang through. Something had suddenly made the crowd uneasy. People stopped talking. Some pointed to the east. Sam climbed a steep wall of rock to about twenty feet above the crowd and shielded his eyes from the sun. Three huge clouds of dust billowed across the desert. The clouds slowly separated and continued toward Petra.

"What is it?" someone said.

A murmur ran through the people in the Siq. "Global Community ground forces!" some shouted. "Keep moving!"

Sam studied the clouds. If those were GC troops, they would be armed. One tank firing into this crowd would leave hundreds dead. Instead of a haven, Petra could become the biggest graveyard in the world.

"Keep moving!" someone yelled from behind.

## Two

# Z-Van's Show

JUDD took a breath and tried to prepare himself as The Four Horsemen bounded onstage. The music was so loud it seemed to penetrate the pores of Judd's skin. The band had an interesting combination of traditional instruments—drums, guitars, even a grand piano—but it also modeled some of the newest musical gadgets.

One woman stood in the middle of what looked like a circular computer screen, reaching out and touching it to play recorded bits of Nicolae Carpathia that beamed onstage and on the giant video screen.

A man with long hair sat on a chair behind Z-Van, moving his hands over a round, drum-like instrument. As the music blared, a huge craft hovered over the audience, casting shadows on the gathering. Whenever the long-haired man slid his hands over the object or beat the instrument, the hovering craft thundered like a cannon.

Video clips of Nicolae Carpathia ran in perfect coordination with the music. The crowd stood in awe as never-before-seen footage of Nicolae's resurrection flashed on-screen.

Z-Van pranced onto the stage, turned to the screen, fell to his knees, and stretched out his arms. "Behold your lord and your god!" he screamed.

The crowd roared its approval.

The video showed a close-up of Nicolae in his glass coffin. The music softened, then grew louder as each instrument pounded in perfect tempo. As the camera pulled back from Nicolae's face, the faint outline of a heart grew red inside his chest. Z-Van fell backward, his feet tucked under him, his head and arms touching the stage.

> "His hands so cold, his heart at rest,
> As lord of all sees one last test.
> A grieving world, we turn to you,
> The one entombed in shadows new."

Nicolae's glowing heart beat with the music, turning from red to gold, then white-hot. Z-Van, still stretched out on the stage, suddenly rose ten feet and hovered, his chest rising and falling with each breath. Judd couldn't see wires or cables holding him.

> *"The planet waits, not knowing when*
> *We'll see this man of love again.*
> *But death is not a worthy foe,*
> *This wound, this sting, he will not go."*

Nicolae's eyes fluttered and the crowd whooped, as if they were experiencing the real thing again. Judd watched, mesmerized by the images, the music, the voices, and the crowd. People with Carpathia's mark lifted their hands and seemed to drink the music like water, as Z-Van reached the chorus of his new song.

> *"Res-urrection, sent from above*
> *Res-urrection, power of love*
> *Res-urrection, rise from your bed*
> *Res-urrection, back from the dead!"*

The chorus built until Z-Van screamed the final words. Nicolae's eyes shot open at that exact moment. The coffin lid flew up, and the great pretender—the fake god who mocked everything good and holy—sat up and looked directly at the camera. The crowd bobbed like an angry ocean as the band unleashed a combination of ear-blistering music and fireworks that exploded above.

Z-Van ripped off his shirt, spread his arms, and rose higher. He stared at the crowd as if in a trance, fireworks bursting around him.

"How's he doing that?" Judd shouted.

Westin shrugged. "It's the first time I've seen him do it. There have to be wires somewhere, but I don't see any."

"Carpathia allowed Fortunato to call down fire," Lionel said. "Could Leon have given Z-Van some kind of weird power?"

"I don't want to think about it," Judd said.

More video flashed on-screen detailing Carpathia's past political "high points." They showed pictures of a young Nicolae and the crowd oohed and ahhed. For an incredible twenty-three minutes, Z-Van flew over the outstretched arms of the people and belted out lyrics in praise to the most evil man on the face of the earth.

When Z-Van finished, someone wheeled a replica of Carpathia onstage, and band members fell to their knees and worshiped it. Like a tidal wave, people in the audience took the cue and dropped to the pavement, some stretching out on their faces, paying homage to Nicolae. Z-Van pointed to his forehead and urged the crowd and those watching via satellite to take the mark as quickly as possible.

When the applause faded, Z-Van took a drink and held the microphone close. "This new album has songs that express the way I feel about the risen potentate. Most of them celebrate his new life and what he's done for us, like the lifting of the boils last night."

People screamed, drowning out Z-Van for a few seconds. Then he continued. "But there's one song on the project that was very difficult to write because not everyone agrees with us about Potentate Carpathia. There are a few who refuse to honor him, who refuse to obey him, and who have come against his efforts for peace."

The crowd booed and some raised fists.

"I met two young people not long ago," Z-Van said, "who tried to convince me that I should buy into their tired, dead religious system. So I wrote a song for them and those like them who may be watching or listening right now. It's called 'What More Does He Have to Do?' "

Judd looked at Lionel. There was no mistaking that Z-Van had written a song about the two of them.

Vicki sat in the middle of the Wisconsin hideout, angry faces turned toward her. Awakening the others had set off a chain reaction. When Mark stumbled out of his room and discovered Vicki had gone outside, his jaw dropped. Colin Dial couldn't believe it either. Becky, Colin's wife, stood behind Vicki and put a hand on her shoulder.

"I thought we made the rules clear," Colin said. "One decision like this affects everybody."

"All right, she made a mistake," Becky said. "Let's not rub her nose in it."

Silence followed. Charlie sat in the corner petting Phoenix, whispering to the dog that he had been a good boy to protect Vicki.

"Who do you think it was?" Shelly said, turning to Tom Fogarty. "Could it have been the GC?"

"Believe me," Tom said, "if the GC knew you guys were here, they wouldn't waste time with cryptic little messages and covering up a couple of cameras. They'd have carted you off to the nearest jail."

"So what does the MM stand for?" Shelly said. "Morale Monitor?"

"It's too crude," Tom said. "Probably somebody's initials."

"If it's not the GC, then who?" Vicki said, glancing at Colin. "Do you have neighbors?"

Colin shook his head. "Not behind us. Just forest for miles. But it has to be someone who knows about our operation. Those cameras were hidden pretty well, and we've been careful not to raise suspicion by doing things outside."

Vicki sighed. "So we have to assume the request is real. Somebody needs help."

"But what kind of help?" Conrad said. "This place is pretty remote. Is somebody being held hostage? Do they need food and a place to stay?"

Maggie Carlson chuckled. "If that's the case, they've come to the wrong place. We're packed in here like sardines."

Jim Dekker, the former satellite operator for the Global Community, walked to the monitor. "I say we put a watch on the sensors twenty-four hours a day. If these people need help, they'll be back."

"What if it's some kind of trap?" Vicki said.

Colin bit his lip. "Why didn't you ask that before you went outside?"

"Don't do that, Colin," Becky said, glaring at her husband. "Vicki has apologized."

Colin nodded. "You're right. But since we're all up, we might as well talk about the overcrowding. I've contacted a friend to the west of us who says they're fixing up an old church camp. It might be ready today."

"Are they believers?" Josey Fogarty said.

"Very strong," Colin said. "It's a mini-teaching community. They read Tsion Ben-Judah's Web site each day and learn as much as they can about the Bible."

"Sounds perfect for newer believers like us," Tom Fogarty said.

"Do we have to go?" Conrad said. "I mean, I'd like to stay active with the kids' Web site and answering questions."

"We're not going to kick anybody out," Colin said. "If you want to stay, you can. This new place is not going to be as high-tech. I think they only have a couple of computers. But it's clear some of us have to move from here. Is anyone interested?"

Sam watched the clouds of dust move closer to Petra. Though Operation Eagle had begun the night before, there were still hundreds of thousands who weren't even close to the narrow entrance to the rock city, and it seemed many would not be able to make it inside.

A man moved to a nearby helicopter, and Sam spotted Micah sitting inside. He knew from Judd and Lionel that this was the famous Dr. Chaim Rosenzweig, but the man had undergone such a complete change that few recognized him.

The chopper rose a few hundred feet, and Sam wondered if Micah was being moved to a safe place. The chopper hovered for a few minutes, then landed.

Sam approached an American with a walkie-talkie. "Can you tell me what's going on?"

"The head of the operation and some others are in there trying to figure out what we should do," the man said.

"What do you mean?" Sam said. "We simply need to get people inside the city of refuge, right?"

"A lot of people here aren't believers. We're worried they won't be protected."

"Then get them inside," Sam said.

"If the GC has rocket launchers, the troops moving this way are within firing range right now. There's probably a bunch of tanks and personnel carriers, from the looks of all the dust being kicked up. If they surround us and fire, it'll be a slaughter." The man squinted at the crowd. "Those troops are minutes away."

"What are we going to do?"

"Only one thing we can do. We'll have to

take up arms against them. We only have a few weapons, but we could hold them off long enough for a few more to make it inside if we start firing before the GC get in position."

The man hurried back to the chopper area. Sam's father had been involved with the military and police operations, but Sam had always been afraid of guns. He had seen what they did to people. But if these innocent, unarmed civilians were about to be fired upon, were they supposed to sit by and let that happen?

Sam dropped to a flat rock and put his face in his hands. "God, I don't believe you've brought us this far just to let the Global Communtiy kill us before we get inside Petra. So I ask you right now to protect all of those who are still outside. Give wisdom to the leaders of Operation Eagle. Don't let anyone fire unnecessarily. Father, guide us in your path, for your glory. Amen."

Sam finished and looked at the chopper hovering overhead. He joined several Israelis nearby who were in an animated discussion.

"I will not take up arms," one man said. "Surely if what we've been told about Messiah is true, he will help us."

"You're a fool if you don't defend yourself," another man said. "I heard that a believer was killed here yesterday. You're going to let them roll right over us with their tanks? It'll be a massacre."

"I didn't say that," the first man said. "I think we should pray. God will help us. Killing Global Community troops is not the answer."

Sam glanced at the crowd and noticed the line had stopped going into the Siq. He moved away from the argument. Wind whipped sand and tiny rocks as the helicopter descended in the distance. Sam angled toward the crowd outside the Siq and found people quiet, unmoving.

"What's wrong?" Sam asked a woman holding an infant.

The woman put a finger to her lips, then motioned ahead. A tall man in a brown robe stood before them. People kept moving back to give the man room. One look at his face and a wave of peace swept over Sam. Was this another prophet sent by God to help overcome the evil of Nicolae Carpathia?

Sam waited with the others, silently, not looking at the clouds of dust, not worrying about weapons or tanks or defending themselves. Sam wondered if this man was an answer to prayer.

## THREE

# Michael

SAM inched closer to the robed man. People had formed a ring around this stranger, standing a few feet back from him. Those who had already gone into the narrow passage waited to see what would happen. Even the helicopters seemed silent.

A group walked onto a giant boulder overlooking the impromptu meeting. As the sound of GC engines grew closer, the man held both hands in the air. Sam expected him to yell so everyone could hear, but he spoke in a normal tone.

"Fear not, children of Abraham. I am your shield. Fear not, for God has heard your voice. He says to you, 'I am the God of Abraham your father: fear not, for I am with you, and will bless you.'"

Sam noticed that people on the far reaches

of the crowd didn't strain or move forward. Everyone was hearing what the man said.

"Behold, the Lord your God has set the land before you: go up and possess it, as the Lord God of your fathers has said unto you; fear not, neither be discouraged. Hear, O Israel, you approach this day unto battle against your enemies: let not your hearts faint, fear not, and do not tremble, neither be terrified because of them; be strong and of a good courage, fear not, nor be afraid of them: for the Lord your God, he it is that goes with you; he will not fail you, nor forsake you.

"Peace be unto you; fear not: you shall not die. Turn not aside from following the Lord, but serve the Lord with all your heart. God your Father says, 'You shall eat bread at my table continually. Be courageous, and be valiant.' Fear not: for they that be with us are more than they that be with them.

"You shall not need to fight in this battle: set yourselves, stand still, and see the salvation of the Lord with you, O Judah and Jerusalem, for the Lord will be with you. God shall hear you, and afflict them because therefore they fear not his name. Say to them that are of a fearful heart, 'Be strong, fear not: behold, your God will come with vengeance, even God with a recompense; he will come and save you.' "

Sam moved a step back as the man approached. Who was he? Was it a man at all?

The crowd made way for him as he walked through, seemingly unfazed by the growing noise from the oncoming war machines. He was a few feet away from Sam when he continued. "For the Lord your God will hold your right hand, saying unto you, 'Fear not; I will help you, people of Israel.' So says the Lord, and your redeemer, the Holy One of Israel.

"Thus says the Lord that created you, O Israel, 'Fear not: for I have redeemed you, I have called you by your name; you are mine.' It shall be well with you. Be glad and rejoice: for the Lord will do great things. The very hairs of your head are all numbered. Fear not therefore: you are of more value than many sparrows.

"The Lord God says, 'Fear not, for I am the first and the last.' Stand firm then, remnant of Israel. Fear not! Fear not! Fear not! Fear not!"

People took up the chant, and voices grew louder as the man walked into the crowd. He made his way to an open area and faced one of the oncoming plumes of dust bearing down on Petra.

Sam turned to an older man next to him. "Do you have any idea who that is?"

"Surely he is sent from the Lord," the man said. "A prophet, perhaps an angel."

Sam nodded. *An angel, not with wings and shimmering clothes, but who speaks words from God and looks like a real man.*

The stranger grabbed his robe at the chest and lifted his face at the advancing armies. Sam felt an incredible sense of peace. He was no longer scared of the Global Community. This was truly God's fight, and God would show himself faithful. The GC troops were a quarter of a mile away and closing in quickly.

Sam moved as close to the man—or angel—as he could and noticed Mr. Stein a few yards away. Sam waved and Mr. Stein nodded, then pointed toward the desert.

For the first time, Sam could see the line of tanks grinding toward them. He could only imagine the most sophisticated weaponry rolling and bouncing closely behind.

Sam ran to Mr. Stein and hugged him. "I'm glad to see you made it," Mr. Stein said. "I want to hear your story of how you got here, but let's watch."

"What's going to happen?" Sam said.

"I believe Michael is going to—"

"Michael? The archangel?"

"Yes, I believe it is him. The Scriptures say he is the protector of Israel." Mr. Stein pointed to the oncoming GC vehicles. "We will either see a display of God's power or they will overrun us."

Judd and Lionel moved back along the edge of the crowd with Westin. "I want to go to the hotel before this place goes wild," Westin said.

"Hang on," Judd said. "Let's hear this song."

Z-Van stepped in front of the video screen, now filled with more images of Nicolae. Some were photos of Nicolae assuming power in Romania. Others included shots of the potentate speaking at the United Nations, in front of crowds in Jerusalem, and poses of him smiling with dignitaries from around the world.

Video of Nicolae killing the two witnesses, Moishe and Eli, ran in the background. Grainy footage appeared of Leon Fortunato calling fire down at Carpathia's funeral.

All this was accompanied by a slow, boomy melody and Z-Van's scratchy voice.

> *"What more does he have to do?*
> *He came back from the dead,*
> *   just like he said.*

*An incredible man with peace and a plan
For a world to be filled with love."*

The song spoke of "two young men, swayed by religion, controlled by a book."

Z-Van continued, yelling now:

*"I've heard this song before.
I've heard about Jesus.
I've heard about sin,
  but he can't solve
  this mess we're in."*

By the end of the verses, Z-Van had the crowd screaming, "What more does he have to do?" Fans went wild when Z-Van strapped himself to two beams of wood and was raised above the stage, mocking the crucifixion of Christ.

Judd shook his head. "I can't stand any more of this."

A block from the gathering, Judd spotted a new loyalty mark application site. GC workers looked like they hadn't slept in weeks. A few people stood in line to be processed. Judd thought about telling them what a mistake they were making, that they were forfeiting their souls, but as he got closer and heard their conversation, he decided against it.

"I'll be able to tell my kids I got the mark

on the day after Nicolae lifted the plague of boils," one woman said.

"Can we hurry it up?" a boy with tattoos and piercings whined. "I want to get back to the concert."

Judd, Lionel, and Westin hurried to the hotel. They would catch the rest of the concert on television.

Sam stared at the oncoming horde. Now he could make out the shapes of rockets on the backs of the second row of vehicles. The noise grew unbearable as the grinding of the tanks and the noise of war bounced off the walls of Petra and shook the earth. Sam shielded his eyes as dust swirled through the air.

Though things looked bad, Sam still felt a strange sense of calm. *This must be what faith is all about,* he thought. *I should be scared to death, scared the GC are going to open fire and blow us up. But I believe God.*

Mr. Stein leaned down. "They're not going to use their weapons on us. They're going to try and run over us."

"And you're not concerned?" Sam said.

"The army that moves before us is controlled by a defeated enemy," Mr. Stein said. "Remember what Michael said. 'Peace be unto you; fear not: you shall not die. Turn not aside from following the Lord, but serve the Lord with all your heart.' "

The tanks chewed up ground only fifty yards away. Grains of sand and tiny rocks skittered like jumping beans at Sam's feet. Michael stood ramrod straight. In fact, most in the crowd hadn't even shielded their eyes from the dust cloud. They had stayed in position, eyes closed, defying the enemies of God to come farther.

Twenty yards.

Sam's heart pounded in sync with the army's advance. He smelled exhaust fumes. Under normal conditions he would have expected screaming, crying, and wailing from the crowd, with people climbing up the side of the rock wall to escape certain death. Instead, no one made a sound.

Ten yards.

How would it happen? What could God possibly do to stop this seemingly immovable force before them? A blaze of fire? A hurricane wind? A wall of water from a rock?

Sam glanced at Michael. His face shone. He was as fierce as a lion, and the angel's courage made Sam's eyes well with tears.

Ten feet!!

Suddenly, thunder pealed. The earth shook with a terrific force. Sam fell to his knees, closed his eyes, and covered his ears. It sounded like the whole world was caving in on itself.

Sam opened one eye and saw an unforgettable sight. The earth, only inches from his knees, had split open. Tanks, rocket launchers, troop carriers, and every GC vehicle tumbled into the chasm. Global Community forces fired in a vain attempt to hurt God's people. Their missiles fell back on top of them and exploded.

Plumes of smoke replaced the dust in the air, and many of the GC vehicles caught fire. Only seconds before, Sam could have stretched out on the ground in front of him. Now, one step and he would fall into a gorge that seemed to have no end.

Sam cringed at the screams and wails of GC troops plunging to their deaths. An aftershock shook the earth, and Sam lost his balance. Mr. Stein grabbed his arm and pulled him from the edge.

Then, as incredible as the opening of the earth had been, another miracle occurred: The walls of the gorge slammed together in front of Sam, sending a spray of dust and rocks into the air. The earth had opened its mouth, swallowed the invading forces, and closed it.

"Incredible," Mr. Stein whispered. "Just like the Red Sea when Moses led the children of Israel out of Egypt."

As the dust settled and the cracking and heaving of the earth came to an end, Sam looked around at the faces of thousands behind him. People were so stunned they couldn't speak. Michael was gone. Sam's eyes stung from the tears that welled up. God had been faithful. He had kept his promise. Every word of Michael's message had been true.

Sam closed his eyes and tears ran down his cheeks. He wished his father had believed. Though his father had been dead for some time, Sam's heart still ached for him. Sam wondered if there were any unbelievers left in the crowd behind him.

Sam wished that for once, Global Community News Network cameras had been on-site to capture what God had done. They would no doubt put Carpathia's spin on the event that had killed hundreds, if not thousands, of GC troops.

Sam turned and saw people still on the ground. Whether out of fear or reverence for God, he couldn't tell, but an eerie silence continued.

Finally, Micah rose and people turned to him. He spoke with a crackling voice, as if he too had been overcome with emotion.

"As long as you are on your knees, what better time to thank the God of creation, the God of Abraham, Isaac, and Jacob? Thank him who sits high above the heavens, above whom there is no other. Thank the One in whom there is no change, neither shadow of turning. Praise the holy One of Israel. Praise Father, Son, and Holy Ghost!"

Sam closed his eyes again and prayed. He felt a hand slip onto his shoulder and smiled. It was Mr. Stein.

# FOUR

# Good-Byes

AFTER a few hours of sleep, Vicki awoke and joined the others in the basement hideout in Wisconsin. Mark and Colin were still upset, so she ate breakfast alone, watching the surveillance cameras on the computer screen.

Colin finally approached her. "I thought you and I would have a look at the area where you were last night. You want to show me?"

Vicki pursed her lips. "Are you going to stay mad at me?"

Colin sighed. "I know you thought you were doing the right thing. I'm upset that you didn't alert us."

"I'm surprised you guys didn't hear the alarm."

Colin nodded. "I need to make it louder and put a monitor in our room. The truth is, with everything that's gone on the past couple of weeks, Becky and I have been praying like crazy for you and your friends. You're almost like family to us, and we wouldn't want to see anything happen to you."

"You've been really kind to take us in," Vicki said. "I'm sorry I messed up."

Colin smiled and asked Mark to watch the cameras and tell them via radio if he saw any movement.

The grass was still wet with dew, and a thick fog rose from the ground as they walked toward the woods. Colin kept an eye on the road as they walked the perimeter of the cameras, making sure no one was watching.

Vicki pointed out where she had found the handkerchief and glove, and Colin retrieved the note. There was nothing written on it except *Help me*, but Colin noticed something strange at the corner of the torn piece of paper. "Take a look at this."

"It looks like a postmark," Vicki said.

"From more than three years ago," Colin said. He pushed the talk button on his radio. "Mark, print out a small sign we can tack to a couple of these trees."

"What do you want it to say?" Mark said.

"Something like, 'We'll help you. Tell us what you need.' Bring that out and ask Becky where we keep the extra surveillance cameras. I want to stick two of them high in the trees so we can see more."

Colin turned to Vicki. "Show me the tree where they tied Phoenix."

Vicki found the right tree and Colin inspected the area. The grass was tromped down, but the dew was heavy and it was difficult to see footprints.

Colin knelt and leaned close to the ground. "Most of this area was untouched by the plague that burned the grass and trees. Anybody who wanted to hide out back in these woods could do it."

"You don't think it's GC?" Vicki said.

"Tom's right. It's not their style," Colin said. "But it still worries me. We'll put up the signs and see if there's any activity tonight."

Vicki started for the house and Colin put out a hand. "We had a meeting before you got up. There are some people leaving today."

"What?" Vicki said.

Colin stared at her. "I'll understand if you want to go with them, but Becky and I agreed you're welcome to stay."

Vicki didn't know what to think. She knew the hideout was crowded, but leaving so soon? She left Colin without speaking and ran to the house. She was surprised to see everyone congregated upstairs in the living room. Tom and Josey Fogarty held clothes Becky had found for them in a storage area. Charlie knelt on the floor with Phoenix by his side.

"How was this decided?" Vicki said.

Becky took a breath and explained that their friend in western Wisconsin, Marshall Jameson, had volunteered to pick up anyone who wanted to move to the campground. "I know this has happened quickly, but we think it's necessary."

Cheryl stepped forward and put a hand on Vicki's shoulder. "I don't know how I can ever thank you for what you did. If I have a girl, the Fogartys have agreed we'll name her Vicki."

Vicki was near tears. "And what if you have a boy?"

"Ryan Victor Fogarty," Cheryl said.

"Are you all going?" Vicki said, finding a seat.

Melinda knelt before her and nodded. "Charlie wants to go if he can take Phoenix. Is that okay with you?"

Vicki looked at Charlie. "Are you sure?"

"Bo and Ginny said they'd take good care of me," Charlie said. "And they're going to put us to work on some more cabins so others can come. Maybe you'll be there someday."

"Yeah," Vicki said. "So who's staying?"

"I am," Shelly said.

"Me too," Conrad said, a sheepish smile on his face. "Mark will stick with us too."

Vicki looked over the faces. So many stories. Melinda, the former Morale Monitor, had become a believer at the schoolhouse. So had Janie. Darrion had known Ryan Daley and almost went back to the start of the Young Trib Force.

"Something tells me this is the right thing to do," Darrion said. "I'll probably miss the high-tech stuff, but maybe there's something new at this place that we're supposed to do."

Vicki wiped her eyes. When she looked at Charlie again, she nearly lost it.

"I promise I'll take real good care of Phoenix," Charlie said.

Vicki nodded. "I know you will. When are you leaving?"

"After dark," Darrion said, "so we have all day to say good-bye."

Judd collapsed on the bed in Westin's hotel room and buried his face in a pillow. He couldn't bear watching the conclusion of Z-Van's concert. What had been billed as a celebration of the end of the plague of sores had become a two-hour commercial for Nicolae Carpathia's mark of loyalty.

The cell phone rang and Judd picked up, thinking it would be Chang with an update from New Babylon. Instead, Judd heard what sounded like singing.

"Judd, it's Sam!"

Judd was overjoyed to hear that Sam was okay and had made his way into Petra. When Sam described his experience with Michael and the GC troops, Judd couldn't believe it. "I haven't heard anything on the news about it."

"You probably won't hear the truth because it's another devastating defeat for the GC," Sam said. "Hang on. There's somebody else here who wants to say hello."

Mr. Stein got on the phone and greeted Judd. Judd told him what had happened to them on their way back to Israel and how Z-Van's plane had been destroyed. "Last time I saw you, you were heading for the choppers outside Masada. Is that how you got to Petra?"

"It's a most incredible story," Mr. Stein said. "Until I saw what the Lord did through Michael, it was the biggest miracle of my life."

"What happened?"

"As you know, the Global Community vehicles rolled up just as we were leaving. I piled into a crowded chopper. We actually had a few more than we should have had."

"Was everyone a believer?" Judd asked.

"I think so," Mr. Stein said. "Some of them

had prayed with Micah that very night. I was glad I was there, along with others, to help answer questions."

"You headed straight for Petra?"

"Yes, but within a few moments it became clear that we were overloaded and the pilot turned back. Three young believers were dropped off at Masada and rushed to get a ride to Petra while the rest of us continued our flight. That's when Global Community forces descended and warned us that we would be shot from the sky if we did not land and surrender."

"What did your pilot do?" Judd said.

Judd could hear the smile in Mr. Stein's voice. "He was a large, black man who had been in the U.S. military. He flashed a bright smile at us and said the only place we would touch down was near the walls of Petra."

"I saw some of the flights get shot at as we drove back toward Jerusalem," Judd said.

"We weren't actually shot at," Mr. Stein said. "Our pilot flew low and tried to avoid any contact with the GC. We were doing well until we flew over a rock formation and came upon a huge firefight. Several GC aircraft fired on Operation Eagle choppers. Our pilot stayed low and hovered in a safe position, inside a narrow rock outcropping.

He hoped we could stay there until the danger passed.

"However, what happened next was incredible. One of the GC choppers above us took a direct hit from another GC aircraft. The bullets literally passed through the Operation Eagle chopper and hit the enemy's helicopter. I saw a flash overhead and the GC aircraft spinning, smoke billowing from its engine, heading straight for us."

"What happened? The pilot must have done something to get out of the way."

"He couldn't move to either side because of the rock formation," Mr. Stein said. "We could only go up or down, and the chopper was hurtling toward us, out of control. The pilot yelled for us to brace ourselves. I wanted to shut my eyes, but something made me keep them open.

"Everything went into slow motion. I could see the rotor blades of the other chopper going round and round, the GC pilot struggling to take control, and then it hit our helicopter."

"The other chopper crashed into yours?" Judd said.

"No, the GC chopper actually passed through our aircraft."

"What do you mean, 'passed through'?"

"In a sense, it was like in the Old Testament

when the Death Angel passed over the houses of the Israelites. The tail section of the GC helicopter passed within inches of my face. I smelled the acrid smoke and felt the rush of wind from the rotor, even heard the screams of those inside the other craft. But the metal and the smoke passed through our aircraft and out the other side without leaving a trace.

"I looked out the window and saw a fireball explode on the rocks below. The others beside me hadn't watched, but I glanced at our pilot and knew from the look on his face that he had seen it too. God protected us in the air, and he gave us protection on the ground today."

Judd talked with Mr. Stein for a few minutes, and then Sam returned. "They have used choppers to airlift people inside the city walls," Sam said. "Many are safely inside, but there is more work to do. They've also brought in supplies and materials so we can build places to sleep and meet. It is a massive operation."

"Won't the GC return?"

"I don't think they know what happened. Hopefully, Operation Eagle can get Tsion Ben-Judah back soon."

When Judd hung up, Lionel came in and plopped onto the bed with a sigh. "Good news and bad news," Lionel said. "The good news is that Z-Van's finally finished. Bad news is that GCNN is reporting that record numbers of people are getting their marks after Z-Van's performance."

Vicki spent the morning with her friends, reliving adventures and listening to stories. Becky, Colin's wife, set up a video camera and recorded the group. Vicki laughed until she cried and cried until she laughed. "Why do any of you have to go?" Vicki said through her tears.

"You know this is the best thing for us and for the Dials," Maggie Carlson said. "Maybe we'll all be together again soon."

One of the most touching moments of the morning came when Charlie choked up about Vicki's influence on his life. "You helped change me," he said. "From the time I was little and all through school, people thought I was retarded. You were the first person who said I could learn just like everybody else. I know I'm still a little slow, but I'm catching up."

Darrion put a hand on Vicki's shoulder. "You helped me through some really tough things in my past I was dealing with. Things that wouldn't let go. And think of all those kids who saw you by satellite during those GC rallies and gave their hearts to God."

"I'll never forget the look on her face when the camera first went on back at the schoolhouse," Conrad said. "Vicki's eyes were about as big as basketballs."

Vicki laughed. "Hey, it was my first time on international television."

"You know, this has to be a little bit of what heaven's going to be like," Janie said. "Not the waiting to leave part, but when we get there, we'll be able to talk about what God's done and how we've helped each other along."

"Without worrying about the next move Nicolae's going to make," Conrad added.

Josey Fogarty sat forward. "I knew from the time I first met Vicki that she and the others had something I didn't. And when people like to characterize teenagers as selfish and consumed with only what they want, you guys cared." She put a hand to her face and her chin quivered. "Tom was only a few minutes away from taking Carpathia's mark when you showed up. You've been an answer to my prayers, even before I knew enough to pray them."

Cheryl hugged Vicki. "We're going to see each other again. And my only prayer is that little Vicki or little Ryan will get to know you, Vicki."

Becky Dial made lunch and the kids talked more. Phoenix barked when someone pulled into the driveway in a fifteen-passenger van.

"It's Marshall," Colin said.

Marshall Jameson was hefty with blond hair and blue eyes. Vicki wondered about his story, but the man got out of the van and rushed inside. "We need to move. Got a tip that the GC are canvassing main roads tonight for anyone without the mark of loyalty. If you're coming to Avery, it has to be now."

The kids who were staying behind helped load the van. Vicki took Phoenix by the collar, hugged him, and helped Charlie get him inside. There were tears and final hugs, and then the doors closed. Vicki covered her mouth with a hand as her friends drove out of sight.

# Five

# Anita's Story

SAM Goldberg found one of the members of Operation Eagle and offered to help. A tall, blond American wearing a flight jacket said they wouldn't be doing more chopper runs from outside. "We're passing out blankets to keep people warm inside and outside the city. Construction will start soon on some of the small buildings."

Sam grabbed an armload of blankets and followed the tanned man. "Do you know where Micah is?"

"I've heard he's alone. Wants to prepare what he's going to say after everybody's settled."

They walked onto a rock outcropping, and Sam got a good look at the people congregated inside Petra. Many sat in small groups, talking. Some looked like they were trying to

convince the undecided about the truth of
God.

The American pointed to a flat location
near the entrance to the Siq. "That's Buck
Williams. He's the one in charge of getting
the building supplies organized."

"The journalist from America?" Sam said.

"Yeah, one of our guys got killed up here
and Buck is taking his place."

Sam handed out the blankets and went
back for another load. He expected people to
be antsy about what was going to happen.
Instead, they seemed grateful for the warmth
of a blanket. Everyone he met thanked him.

On one of his runs for more blankets, Sam
noticed two women talking with a group of
Israelis. He stopped and realized it was Leah
Rose and Hannah Palemoon, the two Opera-
tion Eagle workers he had met on the ride to
Petra.

". . . so we're looking for people who know
about computers who could help us set up a
station."

An older man waved a hand. "Try some of
the young ones. I don't know enough about
computers."

"I know someone," Sam said. "Naomi
Tiberius. She's a teenager, but—"

"That's not important, Sam," Leah said,
smiling. "We're trying to set up some

computer equipment, but we need someone who knows her stuff."

"Naomi would be perfect," Sam said. "She's taught adults how to use programs before. We used to attend the same synagogue."

"And you're sure she's here?"

"I just gave her and her father a blanket. Come on. I'll show you."

Sam led the two to Naomi and her father, Eleazar Tiberius. Naomi spoke only Hebrew, but Leah and Hannah understood her in English. Eleazar seemed reluctant to let his daughter go with the Americans at first, but he soon agreed when he heard about what she would be doing.

Naomi told the two her experience. "I've taught some introductory classes and helped with a couple of networking projects. One for a small business and the other for the science department at the university."

"You're just who we're looking for," Leah said. "We're bringing in a whole set of computers that will allow people here to keep in touch with the Tribulation Force."

Naomi asked how they would get power and several technical questions Sam didn't understand. The women didn't seem to understand them either.

"All we know is, once we get the computers going, our contact in New Babylon will tell you what you need to know."

"What else will the computers be used for?" Naomi said.

"It was David Hassid's hope that we could train Israeli believers to answer questions that come to the Trib Force Web site," Hannah said. "Eventually there should be thousands of computers for mentors to use to reach people around the world."

"And that will all be coordinated through New Babylon?" Naomi said.

"Yes. Chang Wong is our contact," Leah said. "You two will no doubt become good friends."

"Where are the computers?" Naomi said.

Leah used her radio and found out a site had been located for the computer building. It would be constructed high enough to look out on the encampment, but not too high that people would have trouble walking to it.

"They'll bring in modular walls to isolate the machines from wind and dust," Leah said.

"How long will that take?" Sam said.

"They can put up a building this size in about an hour, depending on how many people help," Leah said. "The individual tents and personal living spaces go up faster than that."

"There are others here who know as much,

if not more, about computers than I do," Naomi said.

"Go find them," Leah said. "We'll need all the help we can get."

Naomi scampered off, and Sam scanned the workers lugging boxes of computer equipment to the site. The first modular units were being laid out on the ground, measured, and put together. This rock-walled city was about to change drastically.

Judd checked outgoing flights and found two headed to the States, but they all agreed it was too risky to try and slip onto them. Westin dialed his contacts and found a comparable plane for Z-Van in Spain. The company said they would fly the plane to Israel if Z-Van decided to purchase or lease it.

"It's not as fancy as that old one," Westin said when he hung up, "but it's better than nothing."

That afternoon, Chang called to give Judd an update on Nicolae Carpathia, who was on his way back to New Babylon. "I can't wait to get home and listen to the bug on the Phoenix 216." Chang paused. "I have something I'd like you to pray about."

"What's up?"

"I just came from a meeting with my boss. He had told me I wouldn't have to be interrogated, but now he says he can't make any exceptions."

"You mean the lie detector?" Judd said.

"Yes. I also hacked into their database. They're giving me a surprise inspection tonight."

"Chang, you have to get out of there!" Judd said.

Judd heard a smile in Chang's voice. "On the contrary, I think I have them right where I want them. Just get as many people to pray about this as possible, okay?"

"I will," Judd said.

Chang hesitated. "There's one more thing. It's my parents."

"Have you talked with them?"

"No. And with all that's going on here, I've hardly had time to think about it. But when I do, I'm tied in knots."

Judd thought about his own parents. They must have known Judd wasn't living for God, even though he went to church and made it seem like he was committed. How difficult had it been for them?

"It's terrible when someone you love doesn't believe," Judd said.

"Not only doesn't believe but wants to follow Carpathia," Chang said. "Fortunately they didn't take the mark while they were here. I've heard my father has been disgusted with what happened in Jerusalem, but the people giving the mark don't care what you believe. They just apply it."

"We'll add your mom and dad to the prayer list," Judd said.

Vicki stayed in her room the rest of the morning, a dull ache in her chest from missing her friends. She had wanted to be with Cheryl when she gave birth. She had wanted to help Janie and Melinda grow. How long had she and Darrion been friends? Now it seemed like they were half a world away.

Shelly knocked and came in. "Conrad said you have an e-mail. I told him not to bother you, but he thinks you should see it."

Vicki followed her into the computer room. Mark had fired up the new cameras, and Vicki was amazed at how much they could see of the forest.

Colin and Becky had cleaned the rooms of the others and found Charlie's notebook. Becky gave it to Vicki. "I doubt we'll be able to get this to him anytime soon. Why don't you keep it?"

Vicki stashed it in her room and returned

to find a printed e-mail from Manny's sister, Anita.

> Vicki and Mark,
> By now you've probably heard about Manny. I tried to stop him, but he wouldn't listen. I'd like to tell you what happened, but I'm scared. Please call me late tonight. I've hidden a phone and can talk then.
> Anita

She included her phone number at the bottom of the message. Vicki read it again and shook her head. "Doesn't sound like Manny convinced her to become a believer."

"Are you going to call her?" Shelly said.

Vicki nodded. "Tonight while I'm on duty with the monitor."

Sam was amazed at how quickly buildings went up in Petra. While several men and women worked on the computer center, others constructed personal dwellings. These were small, prebuilt rooms big enough for a bed and perhaps some computer equipment and a dresser or a desk. Younger people gravitated to a lower area where tents had been set up.

Sam loved the atmosphere of the city with people helping each other. Tiny children had to be kept from the edges of cliffs, and several teenagers volunteered to take care of the little ones while parents set up their new homes.

Some started campfires to cook meals, and the crackling fires, along with the smoke that wafted skyward, gave Sam the feeling of being in Old Testament days. And why not? Though their enemies used high-tech weapons, these were no different than the stories of the Philistines in King David's day. Instead of walking around the enemy walls seven times, like Joshua did, the angel Michael had opened a gigantic chasm in the earth.

Sam found Mr. Stein and his new friends, Rabbi and Mrs. Ben-Eliezar, and helped them put together their dwelling. Rabbi Ben-Eliezar asked about the progress of the computer setup, and Sam told them. "We've been trying to call our sons to let them know we are safe but haven't gotten through. We thought we could e-mail them," the rabbi said.

"They should have the system up and running soon," Sam said.

The Ben-Eliezars had many more questions that Mr. Stein answered as they worked together. Sam wandered off when they finished, wondering when Micah would speak.

Vicki took over her four-hour shift monitoring the perimeter of Colin's property at 10 P.M., Wisconsin time. She pulled up the kids' Web site as she watched and read some of the new e-mails. Shelly, Conrad, and Mark were answering as many as they could, but there was no way to keep up with all the questions.

After two hours of nothing but wind blowing through the trees on the monitor and an occasional deer, Vicki dialed Anita Aguilara's number. The phone rang only once before Anita picked up. "Hello?" she whispered.

Vicki identified herself and the girl sighed with relief. "I haven't slept since they killed Manny. In fact, I don't know if anybody here has."

Vicki had prayed for Manny's sister since they first met. "Tell me what happened."

Anita took a breath. "Manny was excited about meeting with Hector and the others. But I saw things Manny didn't. The guys took loaded guns to the meeting."

"So it was a setup?" Vicki said.

"Yes. I don't think they ever wanted to know what had changed Manny's life."

"Did you listen to Manny?"

"Yes. I couldn't believe how much he had learned about God in such a short time."

"That's one of the things God does when you believe," Vicki said. "He gives a desire to learn more about him. What happened in the meeting?"

"Manny was explaining that you can't get to heaven by trying to do good things or work off your sins. Hector laughed and said he didn't want to go to heaven, that all his friends were in hell. That made the others laugh. But Manny didn't let them get to him. He kept going.

"Soon one of the guys became angry. Manny told him he was simply repeating what Jesus said in the Bible. That's when I got confused."

"What confused you?" Vicki said.

"Manny believed that Jesus paid the penalty and had served the sentence for our sin. He said there was only one way to be forgiven and go to heaven, and that's when the guys stood and took him away. They said they had heard enough."

"What did you do?"

"I followed. Manny looked at me and

I think he wanted me to stay away, but I hid in the garage and watched."

Vicki felt a chill run down her spine. She remembered the feeling in that garage and wondered if anyone had ever been killed there.

"What did they do?" Vicki said.

Anita began crying. "Hector took him to the middle of the room and accused him of telling the Global Community too much information. Manny swore he didn't tell them anything."

"He should have come back with us," Vicki muttered.

"Hector held a gun up and told him he had to confess. Manny looked him in the eye and—I'll never forget this—he told Hector the reason he had come back was to tell them the truth about God."

"That's true," Vicki said.

"Manny pleaded with them to ask God to forgive them. He begged them not to take the mark of Carpathia."

Anita broke down and sobbed. When she had composed herself, she whispered, "Hector and the others took turns kicking and beating him. Finally, they all aimed their guns at him and fired. There was nothing I could do."

Vicki shuddered. "Of course there wasn't.

Those men are killers, and you should get out of there."

"They don't know that I saw," Anita said, "but I think Hector wants to get rid of me."

Vicki wanted to hop in a car and rescue Anita that night, but she knew she couldn't. "The most important thing now is for you to believe what Manny was telling you."

"I want to believe," Anita said, "especially after what happened next."

"What's that?" Vicki said.

"After they shot him, they opened a trunk of a car to dump his body. I was crying so hard, I could hardly control myself. And then I heard it. Singing or some kind of noise above. There was a bright light, and the gang members covered their eyes. After a few moments, it went away, but all of the gang members were spooked by it."

Goose bumps ran down Vicki's arms. She had never heard of such a thing happening. Could there have been angels in the room when Manny had been killed?

"What was it?" Anita pleaded. "Can you tell me, Vicki?"

"I don't know for sure. But I do know you can see Manny again."

"How? How can I see him again if he's dead?"

# SIX

# Lie Detector Test

VICKI took a breath and wondered what she could add to Manny's message. Before she could speak, Anita said, "There's something I haven't told you. The guys said they should never have let you and Mark go. They're looking for you."

Vicki ran a hand through her hair. It was enough to have the Global Community on their trail and some crazy, stringy-haired intruder. Now a gang was after the kids too.

"I don't think they'll ever find us," Vicki said. "What's important is for you to understand what Manny was telling you."

"How can I see Manny again?"

"You know all about joining a gang, right? When you're accepted, you take the mark of that gang and become one of them. It's the same with God, only a lot better. When you ask God to forgive you for the bad stuff you've done, he makes you part of his family. But he doesn't make you pass any tests to get in."

"But I have to do something to get him to love me, don't I?"

"No. The Bible says God loves you so much that he gave his only Son. Even before you were born, Jesus died for you, so tell God you believe and you want him to come into your life and forgive you. Do it now."

"Will I see Manny again in heaven?" Anita said.

"Right. He's with Jesus now, and God considers him one who laid down his life for his friends."

"I want to ask God to forgive me," Anita whispered. "But how do I—"

The phone crackled, and Vicki heard something in the background. Anita put the phone down.

"I heard you talking," a male voice said.

"I was just thinking about Manny and crying."

"Why don't you forget him? He's gone."

Vicki recognized Hector's voice. The cold-blooded killer was back.

"We need your help finding those other two. Our GC contact said they escaped the hotel. Will you help us find them?"

"Of course," Anita said. Then she broke down.

"You need time. I understand," Hector said. He was farther from the phone now, and Vicki figured she had pushed it under the pillow. "We'll talk again in the morning."

"Yes," Anita sobbed.

The door closed and Anita picked up the phone. "Did you hear that? Do you see what kind of pressure I'm under?"

"I know," Vicki said. "We can help you get away. Just pray with me."

Anita softly repeated everything Vicki said.

"God, I'm making a choice for you and against everything else. I believe only you have the power to save my soul, and I ask you to come into my life right now. I do believe Jesus died in my place and he really did come back to life so I could spend eternity with you. Forgive me for all the bad things I've done. I ask you to save me from my sin and be my leader from now on. In Jesus' name. Amen."

When Anita finished praying, Vicki congratulated her. "I wish I could see your face right now so you could see my mark and I could see yours."

"One day we'll see each other again," Anita

said. Someone knocked at her door, and Anita whispered that she had to go.

"Call me back when you can," Vicki said. "We'll figure out a way to help you."

Vicki hung up and looked at the clock. It was still more than an hour before Conrad would relieve her at the monitor, but she had to tell someone the good news.

An alarm pierced the night. She looked at the computer and spotted someone tearing paper from a tree and running away.

Lionel watched the Global Community News Network while Westin met with Z-Van and Judd checked in with the Young Trib Force. A crowd had gathered in New Babylon, awaiting the arrival of Potentate Carpathia and his senior cabinet. Footage of the event would run throughout the evening.

Carpathia pulled up to the palace in a limousine, and several hundred Peacekeepers in full dress uniform formed a phalanx for him to walk through. Lionel guessed it was to convince the world that Nicolae was still in control, even though Lionel knew the Global Community had lost hundreds, if not thousands, of troops in the night.

Commentators didn't mention the terrible

losses in the desert. Also absent from the coverage was news of the devastation of the oceans that teemed with blood. Sea creatures as well as human beings caught on the ocean had died, but the GC hailed this as a time of celebration.

Several people stepped out of the limo, including a silly-looking Leon Fortunato complete in his Most High Reverend Father garb. Leon slowly made his way to a microphone at the bottom of the velvet-lined stairs.

When the crowd quieted, Leon raised a hand. "Thank you for that wonderful display of affection. The world now knows who it was in Israel's temple, who has command over the stars as well as our very flesh. We owe everything to our lord and king, especially our worship."

The crowd applauded and Leon yelled over the noise, "Israel is truly the Holy Land, because Nicolae Carpathia has been installed as the true and rightful god!"

The crowd roared, and Leon gathered his robe and beamed at the audience. Suddenly, a man at the back of the crowd called, "What about the oceans? What does the potentate say about all the blood—"

Before he finished his sentence, several Peacekeepers wrestled the man to the ground. Leon simply smiled at the interruption. "In the fullness of time, all things will become evident. These momentary interruptions in our lifestyles will one day be explained, and we will find the answer to all of our questions in the one we worship.

"I urge you to watch the events of the coming days and see the majesty and splendor of our great god and king. Offer him your praise, your adoration, and your very lives as he has so willingly offered his own for you. And do not delay in taking the loyalty mark. There are now more application sites than ever before for your convenience. Take the mark and your lives will continue in peace." Leon's face contorted. "Refuse the mark and your lives will never be the same."

Lionel stared at the screen as Leon backed away from the microphone and climbed the steps. As the camera pulled back to show the entire palace, lightning flashed in the background. Lionel said a prayer for Chang Wong.

Vicki told everyone what had happened with Anita. The kids prayed for her and asked God to help her get away from Hector's gang.

Colin played and replayed the grainy footage at the edge of the woods. The sight of the darkly dressed stranger creeping through the tree line frightened Vicki. The kids debated whether it was a male or female for several minutes, but they finally concluded there was no way to tell.

Colin switched back to the live camera shots and sat by the monitor. "Whoever this is, I don't think they're trying to hurt us. It's clear they could have done that a long time ago. But it's not a good thing to have people traipsing around out there."

"What do you think we should do?" Conrad said.

"Sleep in tomorrow morning," Colin said. "We'll head out at night and see if we can't catch an intruder."

The phone rang and Judd was glad to hear from Chang. It was evening in New Babylon and Chang seemed excited. "They came to my apartment tonight," he said.

"Who?" Judd said.

"Two uniformed Peacekeepers. They found my laptop, but of course they couldn't find anything on it. I kept an attitude toward the guy and he didn't like it, which is good."

"What do you mean?" Judd said.

"I'm trying to play things cool with my

superiors. You know, not seem too excited about working here. Just do my job. That way, they don't suspect me of being a mole."

"And how did they respond?" Judd said.

"The guy who tried to give me the lie detector test was pretty ticked," Chang said.

"They gave you the test? What happened?"

"I refused to take the test until my boss, Mr. Figueroa, showed up. He asked me a series of yes-or-no questions. Is today Sunday? Are you a male? That kind of thing. When he asked if I was loyal to the supreme potentate, I closed my eyes and reminded myself that Jesus Christ is the one who fits that description, and I answered yes."

"So you passed?" Judd said.

"The test went on for some time. I had to evade a couple of answers that could have hurt me, but I think I passed."

"But they could come knocking on your door at any minute and haul you away."

Chang sighed. "I suppose. But I feel a sense of purpose in what I'm doing. God has put me here. And if that is true, he can protect me from anything the evil one has planned. Plus, David Hassid trusted me with this assignment. I don't want to let him down."

"You know Carpathia is back in New Babylon."

"Yes, and you should have heard the recording from his plane. After Figueroa left, I got my laptop working again with a special code I've programmed into it. I listened to the recording of Carpathia, but there's one part I don't understand. Let me play it for you."

Judd listened as Chang punched a few buttons.

Carpathia's voice sounded over the noise of his airplane. "Leon, please! You have conferred upon your underlings the power I have imbued you with, have you not?"

"I have, Your Worship, but I prefer not to refer to them as underl—"

"Have any of them, one of them—you, for instance—come up with a thing to match the oceans-to-blood trick?"

Chang stopped the recording. "Who are the underlings Carpathia's talking about?"

"I don't know, but I'd love to hear what Dr. Ben-Judah would say to that," Judd said. "What else does Carpathia say?"

"He chews Leon out for the fiasco on the oceans. He gets mad at Viv Ivins for trying out his throne in Jerusalem, and then he has everybody take a lie detector test. Everybody passes, even the stewards. Then Carpathia has Supreme Commander Akbar give him the test. Listen to this."

Judd heard a click, then Akbar's voice, followed by Carpathia's.

"State your name."

"God."

"Is today Sunday?"

"Yes."

"Is the sky blue?"

"No."

"Are you a male?"

"No."

"Do you serve the Global Community?"

"No."

"Are you loyal to the citizens under your authority?"

"No."

"Have you ever done anything disloyal to the Global Community?"

"Yes."

"Do you leak confidential information to someone inside GC headquarters that undermines the effectiveness of your cabinet?"

"No. And I would personally kill anyone who did."

"Did you rise from the dead, and are you the living lord?"

"Yes."

"Can the Global Community count on your continuing loyalty for as long as you serve as supreme potentate?"

"No."

"You astound me, Excellency."

"Well?"

"I don't know how you do that."

"Tell me!" Carpathia said.

"Your answers all proved truthful, even where you were obviously sporting with me and saying the opposite of the truth."

"The truth is what I say it is, Suhail. I am the father of truth."

A chill passed through Judd as he listened to the father of lies. "I still say you should get out of there, Chang."

Chang sighed. "I say, let the dragon roar. One day the world will see that his is the squeak of a tiny mouse compared with the True Potentate."

Sam Goldberg heard the whir of the chopper blades outside Petra and climbed to a high place for a better look. Members of the Tribulation Force preparing to leave stood together with Micah. Many of the overflow crowd of Israelis had moved outside Petra and camped there.

Sam had been told by one of the Americans that the Tribulation Force was on its way back to the States to retrieve Dr. Tsion Ben-Judah. The group joined hands, and then Micah appeared to pray for them. Sam wished he was close enough to hear. He longed for Micah to speak to those assembled in Petra. Sam hoped the moment was close.

# SEVEN

# Sam's Meeting

VICKI tossed and turned, thinking of Anita. Who knew what Hector would do to her if he found out she had become a believer? The more Vicki stewed about the situation, the more she became convinced that she had to do something quickly. She found Shelly awake and they went over their options.

"You know we can't go back there," Shelly said. "Colin wouldn't go for it, and between the gang people and the GC, it'd be too dangerous."

"What if we asked somebody else to go get her?" Vicki said.

"Who? Everybody we know is on the other side of Wisconsin."

"How about Carl Meninger?"

"In South Carolina?" Shelly said. "Chicago's a long way from there."

Vicki snapped her fingers. "How about one of the believers from the schoolhouse?"

"Lenore!" Shelly shouted, then covered her mouth.

Vicki stood and raced into the media room where Becky watched the monitor. Vicki described their plan, and Becky agreed it was a good one.

As far as Vicki knew, Lenore had contacted the Young Trib Force only twice since they had escaped the schoolhouse. She found an e-mail Lenore had sent shortly after leaving the kids. Lenore and Tolan, her infant son, along with a few others from the school-house, had moved from Lenore's house to an abandoned community center in the Chicago suburb of Bolingbrook. In a second e-mail a few weeks later, Lenore explained that people had restored the building, and they were looking forward to bringing others in also.

Vicki typed an e-mail and asked Lenore to call her as soon as possible. She didn't want to explain too much about the situation in case someone else was screening Lenore's messages.

Before Vicki's head hit the pillow, the phone rang. Lenore was ecstatic to hear from Vicki and wanted to know everything that had happened to her.

"How did you get the message in the middle of the night?" Vicki said.

"We have someone watching our e-mail at all hours. There are people who will warn us about possible GC raids. They woke me when they saw your message."

Vicki described their adventure with the GC, their travels in Wisconsin and Iowa, and broke the news about the deaths of their friends Pete Davidson and Natalie Bishop.

Lenore gasped. "I'd heard that some people chose the guillotine instead of Carpathia's mark, but it's hard to believe your friends are gone."

"Yeah, and there's a new believer who needs our help, but our hands are tied."

"What do you need?" Lenore said.

Vicki told Lenore about Anita. "I'm not being dramatic when I say that this is proba-bly the most dangerous thing we could ask you to do."

"If it means safety for a fellow believer," Lenore said, "consider it done."

"What about Tolan?" Vicki said.

"He has a lot of people here who care for him. There are even two young men staying here who play with Tolan. You should see him. He's growing so fast."

Vicki took down Lenore's number and said

she would call as soon as Anita contacted them.

"Tell that girl I'm coming to get her as soon as she gives the word," Lenore said. "And you stay safe up there."

Judd joined Lionel and told him what had happened to Chang. As they discussed GCNN news coverage and watched a replay of clips from Z-Van's concert, Westin walked in. His face was ashen.

"You look like you've seen a ghost," Lionel said.

Westin fell into a chair, and Judd turned off the television.

It took Westin a few moments to compose himself. "I just met with Z-Van about the new plane."

"What did he say?" Judd said.

"He's buying it and having it flown here tomorrow. I'm hoping to still give you guys a ride home."

"That's great," Lionel said. "So why are you so upset?"

Westin squinted. "Something's happened to Z-Van. Maybe it was what the concert did—his new album is number one and they haven't even released it yet."

"What do you mean?" Judd said. "His looks have changed?"

Westin shifted in his chair. "The guy has always been into weird, dark stuff, but something's happened. His eyes are vacant, like Z-Van's not really there anymore."

Judd told Westin what Chang had overheard on Carpathia's plane. "You think Leon could have given Z-Van power to levitate above the stage like that?"

"I guess it's possible." Westin smirked. "That's all we need—more little Carpathias running around."

"You're saying Z-Van is under somebody else's control?" Lionel said.

"Maybe he took some drugs, or he was energized by the concert," Westin said, "but it sure seemed like I was talking to a different person."

Judd shivered. If Z-Van had been given power by Fortunato, could Judd and the others risk being around him? Z-Van knew he and Lionel were believers. Would he try to zap them?

Sam had watched most of the American Tribulation Force, as well as members of Operation Eagle, leave Petra. He felt sad that they

wouldn't be able to experience the peace
and safety he and the other Israelis felt.
Impromptu prayer gatherings had sprung up
throughout the different camps. Young and
old asked God to convince those who still
hadn't believed that Jesus Christ was the true
Messiah.

Sam was amazed at the progress on the
communications center Naomi Tiberius
was putting together. Hundreds of boxes
filled with computer equipment perched
on rocks near the building. Sam hoped he
would be among the first allowed inside to
read the latest from Tsion Ben-Judah. It felt
like a year since he had seen the man's
Web site.

Sam thought of the millions of believers
around the world who had no safety. They
were now in the Great Tribulation, a period
of three and a half years of intense persecu-
tion and death. Sam knew those who
wouldn't take the mark of Carpathia would
be hunted down like animals. No one on
earth had survived the past three and a half
years without knowing someone who had
died. The next three and a half years would
be even worse.

Sam wandered about the camps, listening
and watching a million people uprooted
from their homes, torn from everything they

knew. So far he hadn't heard complaining, and he wondered how long that would last.

He found a flat rock near a newly constructed dwelling and sat on it, looking out at the scene. To his surprise, out of the small building came Micah. Sam felt like he was intruding and tried to quietly slip away.

"You there," Micah said, "where are you going?"

"I didn't know . . . I mean, I don't want to disturb you, sir."

Micah smiled, his long robe flowing in the slight breeze. "Come and sit with me."

Sam couldn't believe he was actually talking to the man. "I'm grateful to you, Mr. Micah, how you stood up to Carpathia."

"Don't thank me. Thank the God who empowered me. He was the one speaking and doing the standing up."

Sam told Micah about his friend Daniel and how Carpathia had murdered him inside the temple. "I was hoping he would become a believer in Christ, but Nicolae killed him."

"We don't know what was in his heart at that moment," Micah said. "He refused a direct order from Nicolae. Perhaps he understood the truth because of something you said."

"I hope that's what happened."

"Yes, hope," Micah whispered, looking out at the gathering. "It's almost like we're in heaven, isn't it? A million people living in harmony. Only God could do that."

"When will you speak to them?" Sam asked.

"When the time is right. If there is one thing I have learned since coming to the truth, it is that I need to wait on God."

"How did you become a believer?" Sam said. "I thought you were a supporter of Nicolae."

"I was. I believed everything he said. It took the plague of locusts, a plane crash, and the continual love of friends to help me understand that Carpathia is a counterfeit. He is not for peace. His goal is war against God. I'm ashamed of myself for being so blind, but God snatched me from my delusion and I praise him for it." Micah looked at Sam. "What about you?"

Sam told him the story of his father and how he had met two teenagers from America who explained the message of Christ.

"You owe them a huge debt," Micah said. "I am sorry about your father. But look around. There are many fathers without sons in this gathering."

"God has given me a good friend in Mr.

Stein," Sam said. He explained how the two had met.

After a few minutes, Micah closed his eyes and drank in the fresh air.

"May I ask you one more thing?" Sam said. "You met with the Americans before they left. What did you tell them?"

Micah rubbed his chin. "I owe much to those people. It is difficult to see them go and not know whether we will ever see each other in this life again.

"There was a dear lady who urged me to take on the mantle God had given. Her name was Hattie. I was reluctant to come here and obey God at first."

"Like Jonah in the Bible."

"Yes, like Jonah. But she challenged me. She said I didn't act thankful that God had chosen me to do something unique, and she was right. I was resigned to what I had to do. I had to work hard not to be a coward facing up to Carpathia."

"That's understandable."

"But you see, when she faced Carpathia, she did so with great courage and an understanding that it was God using her. Until that day, I was only focusing on what would happen to me. She had the right attitude."

Micah leaned back and put both hands

behind him. "While we were still at the safe house in America, she told me God was going to do great things through me and that she would be praying for me every step of the way. I will never forget her."

Sam noticed a twinkle in Micah's eyes. The man stood and looked at one of the high places above them. "I gave an urn to my friends to take back to America. We do not worship the remains of those who die, but my hope is that one day we will be able to toss Hattie's ashes to the winds here in Petra—as an act of worship to the one true God. Hattie would have wanted that. They'll bring her ashes back when they return with Tsion Ben-Judah, who will address the remnant of Israel."

"I can't wait for that," Sam said, reaching out to shake Micah's hand.

Micah grabbed Sam's arms tightly. "Neither can I, my friend." He paused and closed his eyes. "I will pray for you the same thing I prayed for our friends from America. 'Now to him who is able to keep you from stumbling, and to present you faultless before the presence of his glory with exceeding joy, to God our Savior, who alone is wise, be glory and majesty, dominion and power, both now and forever. Amen.'"

Judd suggested they ask God for wisdom,
and Lionel and Westin joined him on their
knees. Lionel began by praising God for his
protection and thanking him for getting
them back to Jerusalem safely. "We don't
know why you've kept us here, Lord, but
there must be some reason. We acknowledge
that your ways are not ours, and we ask you
right now for wisdom on what to do."

After a few minutes, the cell phone rang
and Judd picked up. It was Chang Wong. "I
think we were wrong about Petra."

"What do you mean?" Judd said.

"Tsion Ben-Judah thought it was a place of
safety, but Nicolae Carpathia is about to level
it with bombs!"

# EIGHT

# Nicolae's Plan

Judd's heart raced. He had assumed Petra truly was a place of safety because of the things that had already happened there. Was there a chance Tsion was wrong?

"What are you talking about?" Judd said to Chang.

"I've been listening to the recorded conversation between Nicolae and his assistants. They're talking about the final solution to the Israeli dissidents and the Judah-ites."

"Final solution? That sounds like World War II and Adolf Hitler's plan to wipe out the Jews."

"That's exactly what Nicolae wants to do."

"Does he know about the defeat of his army?" Judd said.

"Not until late on the recording when they near New Babylon. Here, I'll play you the part where Nicolae is talking to Suhail Akbar."

Judd heard a couple of computer clicks, then a whirring noise from the plane.

"Answer my question, Suhail."

"Yes, of course, but I have bad news."

"I do not want bad news! Everybody was healthy! We had plenty of equipment for the Petra offensive. You were going to ignore the city—waiting to destroy it when Micah and Ben-Judah were both there—and overtake those not yet inside. What could be bad news? What do we hear from them?"

"Nothing. Our—"

"Nonsense! They were to report as soon as they had overtaken the insurgents. The world was to marvel at our complete success without firing a shot, no casualties for us versus total destruction of those who oppose me. What happened?"

"We're not sure yet."

"You must have had two hundred commanding officers alone!"

"More than that."

"And not a word from one of them?"

"Our stratospheric photo planes show our forces advancing to within feet of overrunning approximately 500,000 outside Petra."

"A cloud of dust and the enemy, in essence, plowed under."

"That was the plan, Excellency."

"And what? The old men in robes and long beards fought back with hidden daggers?"

"Our planes waited until the dust cloud settled and now find no evidence of our troops."

Judd had to smile as Carpathia laughed. The evil man had no idea his troops had been swallowed by the desert.

"I wish I were teasing you, Potentate," Akbar said. "High-altitude photographs ten minutes after the offensive show the same crowd outside Petra, and yet—"

"None of our troops—yes, you said that. And our armaments? One of the largest conglomerations of firepower ever assembled, you told me, split into three divisions. Invincible, you said."

"Disappeared."

"Can those photographs be transmitted here?"

"They're waiting in your office, sir. But people I trust verify what we're going to see . . . or not see, I should say."

Carpathia sounded like he was ready to explode. "I want the potentate of each of the world regions on his way to New Babylon within the hour. Any who are not en route sixty minutes from now will be replaced. See to that immediately, and when you determine when the one from the farthest distance will arrive, set a meeting for the senior cabinet and me with the ten of them for an hour later." Carpathia paused and slowly said, "And these Jews, we expect them all to be in Petra as soon as they can be transported there?"

"Actually, they will not all fit. We expect Petra itself to be full and the rest to camp nearby."

"What is required to level Petra and the surrounding area?"

"Two planes, two crews, two annihilation devices. We could launch a subsequent missile to ensure thorough devastation, though that might be overkill."

"Ah, Suhail. You will one day come to realize that there is no such thing as overkill. Let the Jews and the Judah-ites think they have had their little victory. And keep the failed operation quiet. We never launched it. Our missing troops and vehicles and armaments never existed."

"And what of the questions from their families?"

"The questions should go *to* the families. We demand to know where these soldiers are and what they have done with our equipment."

"Tens of thousands AWOL? That's what we will contend?"

"No, Suhail. Rather, I suggest you go on international television and tell the GCNN audience that the greatest military effort ever carried out was met by half a million unarmed Jews who made it disappear! Perhaps you could use a flip chart! Now you see us; now you do not!"

Judd felt a mix of joy and fear. He was glad Nicolae finally realized he had lost this battle to God and his followers. But if Carpathia tried to destroy Petra from the air, would it work? Surely those old walls couldn't withstand the power of the GC missiles.

The next day Vicki received the call from Anita they had all been waiting for. She had convinced the other gang members that she wouldn't run, that there was no need to leave.

"Did Hector ask you about what they had done to your brother?" Vicki said.

"I told them Manny got what he deserved," Anita said. Then her voice broke. "Can God forgive me for saying such a thing?"

Mark got Lenore on the phone as Vicki talked with Anita. He covered his phone and said, "Lenore thinks she can be there in an hour, hour and a half tops."

Anita said she had access to a fire escape outside a third-floor window that was left unguarded. Lenore gave the make and color of the compact car she would be driving and hung up.

"Keep the cell phone with you and set it to vibrate," Vicki said. "When Lenore gets close, I'll call you."

Sam helped Naomi and others move computer equipment into the new communications building in Petra. He kept the conversation with Micah to himself, smiling as he moved around the crowded room.

While Naomi set up the complex network of equipment, Sam found a satellite laptop one of the Operation Eagle members had left behind and visited the kids' Web site, theunderground-online.com. Over the past few months he had felt connected to other kids around the world by visiting the Web site and reading the latest postings from Tsion Ben-Judah.

A flashing message greeted him as he opened the Web site. He had seen it a couple of times before when someone was in serious trouble.

*Please pray for a believer in the States
who is in danger. One believer has already
lost his life at this location. We don't feel
we can be any more specific, but please pray
that God would allow this person to escape
and relocate with other believers.*

*Sincerely,
The Young Trib Force*

Sam wondered if the Global Community
had caught someone. No matter what the
problem was, Sam knew prayer was the best
thing he could do from the other side of the
world. He called Naomi and a few others
over. In a makeshift computer room in
Petra, seven people knelt on the hard floor
and prayed for a believer they didn't know,
in a situation none of them could imagine.

Vicki jumped when the phone rang. It was
Judd, saying he had seen the alert on the
Web site and wanted to know if everything
was all right. Vicki explained the situation
with Anita and said they were waiting for
Lenore's call.

"I won't keep you, then," Judd said.

"Wait. Where are you?" Vicki said.

Judd gave her a quick update about what had happened with Z-Van's plane and the concert. "It was awful, Vick. The guy even wrote about Lionel and me in one of his songs."

"Any idea when you'll get a flight out of there?"

"You don't know how psyched we were to be coming home. We're hoping to come home on this new plane, but we can't say for sure."

"Let us know when you're headed back so we can have someone meet you," Vicki said.

"Okay. I hope everything works out for Anita. We'll be praying."

Thirty minutes after Judd hung up, Vicki took a call from Lenore. She thought she was close to the hideout. Vicki located Lenore's position on a map Mark had pulled up on the computer screen. "You're really close. Go another two blocks and pull over."

Vicki explained what the building looked like as Mark dialed Anita on another phone.

"I see it," Lenore said. "I'm pulling over."

"Look for a fire escape," Vicki said.

Mark handed the other phone to Vicki. "Anita's moving upstairs," he said.

With a phone to each ear, Vicki took a deep breath. "Anita, are you at the fire escape?"

"Almost there," Anita said, out of breath.

"Which side of the building is the escape on?" Lenore said. "I don't see it."

"Where's the fire escape, Anita?" Vicki said.

"On the back side," Anita said. "At the alley."

Vicki relayed the message and Mark said, "We should just have them talk to each other."

"Good idea, but too late," Vicki said.

"What?" Anita and Lenore said in unison.

"Nothing . . . Anita, where are you?"

"I'm at the window, third floor."

"Lenore?"

"Coming around the corner. I see the fire escape."

"Okay," Vicki said. "Anita, go!"

"I can't get the window open," Anita said.

"I see a couple of people back here," Lenore said.

"I got it open! I'm moving out now."

"Wait," Vicki said. "Lenore, who do you see?"

"Two guys. They're looking up. I'm stopping now. I'm right under the escape."

"Anita, don't go out yet," Vicki said.

"I'm already . . ." Anita's voice trailed off.

"What is it?" Vicki said.

Tires squealed and Vicki heard a pop, pop, pop. She couldn't tell which phone it had come from. Maybe both. Glass crashed and someone screamed.

"Anita? Lenore?" Vicki shouted.

"They just shot her windshield," Anita said. "She's backing up the alley, and they're running after her . . . what should I do?"

Vicki felt short of breath. "Lenore, what's going on?"

Lenore didn't answer, but Vicki heard the revving engine of the small car.

"I'm going down anyway," Anita said. "The guys are chasing the car on foot, and they've gone around the building."

"Lenore, talk to me!" Vicki screamed.

Suddenly Lenore came back on the line, out of breath. "I had to drop the phone! Tell Anita I'm coming around the other way!"

Vicki relayed the message as Anita reached the bottom of the fire escape. "Here she comes!"

Tires screeched and Vicki heard the door open. "Get in!" Lenore yelled. The engine revved again and Anita's phone banged loudly.

"Floor it!" Anita yelled. Then another pop, pop, pop. Screams. Lenore's phone went dead.

"Lenore? Anita?" Vicki said.

The room fell silent. Vicki listened to Anita's phone and heard voices and people running, but no one answered. She tried to explain what she had heard to the others. Shelly fell into a chair and put her head in her hands.

"Maybe they're okay," Conrad said.

Mark clenched his teeth and stared at the computer screen.

"What?" Vicki said. "You think we shouldn't have gotten Lenore involved?"

Mark looked away. "I was just thinking of Tolan. If his mother doesn't come back—"

A male voice spoke into Anita's phone. "Who is this?"

Vicki was so startled, she blurted out, "Vicki Byrne. Who's this?"

"So you're trying to help your little friend escape?"

Vicki covered the phone and looked at Mark. "It's Hector."

"I should have taken care of you while I had the chance," Hector muttered. A mechanical grating sounded in the background. A garage door was opening. A siren wailed in the distance.

"Don't worry," Hector said. "We'll track them down. They won't live long. And neither will you."

# NINE

# Shattered Glass

VICKI thought of Tolan waiting at home for his mother. She would never forgive herself if that little boy had to go through the rest of the Tribulation alone. But was she supposed to let Anita stay with gang members who would eventually hurt her? Vicki looked around the room, but everyone seemed to be staring at the floor.

"Lenore's phone cut out, right?" Conrad said. "Call her back."

Shelly looked up. "But what if the gang guys caught up to them?"

"Let's find out," Conrad said.

Vicki's hands trembled as she punched in Lenore's number. It rang once, and then someone picked up. Wind whooshing through the car blasted in Vicki's ear. "They're still moving," she said.

"Hello?!" Anita said.

"Anita! It's Vicki. Where are you?"

"Vicki, I can't believe it! I see it! You were right. I see it!"

"See what?" Vicki said.

"The cross! The mark of the true believer! It's right there on Lenore's forehead like you said."

Vicki put a hand over the phone and told the others. "Anita, are you all right?" she said.

"Yes," Anita shouted. "They shot out our windshield and back window, but we're still going."

"Hector must have picked up your phone because I just talked to him," Vicki said. "The gang members are coming after you."

Anita relayed the message to Lenore, and the woman grabbed the phone. "I don't think we can outrun these guys. Got any ideas?"

"Where are you?" Vicki said.

Lenore gave their location, and Mark looked it up on the map. "Okay, right turn at the next intersection," he shouted.

Tires squealed, and it sounded like Lenore hardly slowed as she rounded the corner.

"Two streets down, take a left," Mark said, pointing out the route to Colin.

An hour later, Mark had successfully navigated them through backstreets until Lenore and Anita made it to the suburb of Elmhurst. Lenore pulled into a secluded parking lot of a college and stopped.

"I can't thank you guys enough for helping me," Anita said. "Lenore says she can find her way back from here."

"Now that Hector has your phone, he'll have our number too," Vicki said.

"The phone was Hector's, and I erased your number from the directory after I called you," Anita said. "They shouldn't be able to find either of us."

Vicki smiled as she thought about Anita dropping the phone before she got in Lenore's car. God was working on her conscience, even in such a desperate situation. "Call us as soon as you get to Bolingbrook," Vicki said.

Judd awoke the next morning in Israel and immediately headed for the computer. He was relieved to see an update from Vicki.

> *Thanks to those of you who prayed. The situation with our friend was resolved, and she is now safe with friends who are helping her learn more about God. Vicki B.*

Judd e-mailed Chang and received a reply a few minutes later.

> *I don't know how Mr. Hassid did this. It's so lonely. I'm praying I'll be delivered or that God will send someone to help me. I haven't seen any other believers in New Babylon.*
>
> *My job right now is to monitor the plague of blood on the seas. The ten regional potentates are with Carpathia now. You know what that meeting is about.*
>
> *There is more bad news for the Tribulation Force. An operation to rescue two teenagers in Greece has gone wrong. Several believers were killed, and the GC captured the pilot who was there to pick them up.*
>
> *I don't know how long I will have to stay here, but I pray nothing like that will happen. God has placed me here for a reason, and I have to stay strong and carry on despite the danger.*

Judd read the last paragraph again, identifying with Chang's feelings. He didn't want to be in Israel, but for some reason he was still here. Would God still use him in some way while he was here?

In the afternoon, Sam found Mr. Stein talking to his new friends, Rabbi and Mrs. Ben-

Eliezar. The couple still hadn't been able to contact their sons. Mr. Stein broke away, and Sam told the man about his discussion with Micah.

Mr. Stein seemed elated. "There is a buzz in the camp," he said. "I believe Micah is going to address everyone this afternoon."

"Our provisions are running low," Sam said. "If there are no shipments of supplies coming in, things will get desperate soon."

"God has promised to provide," Mr. Stein said.

As Sam walked through the settlements, everyone in Petra seemed in good spirits. Even those who had camped outside didn't complain. Sam moved through the Siq to the area where the Global Community army had been swallowed by the earth. There was no trace of tank tracks, guns, ammunition, or even spent cartridges. The ground looked as if it had never been touched.

As Sam was going back inside, he noticed a lone figure standing on a rock high above Petra, where he could be seen by those inside and outside the city.

Micah! He was finally going to speak to everyone, and Sam would be too far away to hear. He raced for the opening of the Siq, but Micah's voice stopped him.

"My friends, stay where you are and listen," Micah said, not yelling or screaming, but speaking softly. Sam could hear, and from the look on people's faces, so could everyone else. "I want to remind you that my colleague and friend Tsion Ben-Judah has promised to come and address you all in person."

A roar that seemed like it would topple the very rocks Micah stood on rose from the crowd and echoed off the walls. "We can't wait!" one man near Sam screamed.

Micah raised a hand and the noise died.

"You know, do you not," Micah said, "that the Word of God tells us we will live here unmolested, our clothes not wearing out, and we will be fed and quenched until the wrath of God against his enemies is complete. John the Revelator said he saw 'something like a sea of glass mingled with fire, and those who have the victory over the beast, over his image and over his mark and over the number of his name, standing on the sea of glass, having harps of God.' Beloved, those John would have seen in his revelation of heaven and who had victory over the beast are those who had been martyred by the beast. Death is considered victory because of the resurrection of the saints!

"Sing with me the song of Moses, the

servant of God, and the song of the Lamb, saying: 'Great and marvelous are your works, Lord God Almighty! Just and true are your ways, O King of the saints! Who shall not fear you, O Lord, and glorify your name? For you alone are holy. For all nations shall come and worship before you, for your judgments have been manifested.'

"John said he heard the angel of the waters saying, 'You are righteous, O Lord, the One who is and who was and who is to be, because you have judged these things.'

"And what," Micah continued, "of our enemies who have shed the blood of saints and prophets? God has turned the oceans into blood, and one day soon he will turn the rivers and lakes to blood as well, giving them blood to drink. For it is their just due.

"But what shall we his people eat and drink, here in this place of refuge? Some would look upon it and say it is desolate and barren. Yet God says that at twilight we shall eat meat, and in the morning we shall be filled with bread. In this way we shall know that he is the Lord our God."

Another cheer rose from the crowd. When Sam looked again, Micah was gone. Sam walked back through the Siq and located Mr. Stein.

They were together that evening when a fluttering of wings sounded overhead. White birds seemed to land where people were congregated and let themselves be caught.

"Pigeons?" Sam said.

Mr. Stein laughed. "Have you never had quail before? It is a delicacy." He gathered a few birds in his arms. "Come, help me start a fire and I will show you."

When the preparation time was over, Sam sat down to a meal of roasted quail. Sam found a place to sleep in the communication building, where Naomi continued networking the computers the Tribulation Force had flown in. He slept with a full stomach, and when he awakened the next morning, people walked around the building, talking and laughing.

Sam walked into the morning sun. People dotted the hillside and rocks, bending over and inspecting something on the ground. Sam climbed onto a nearby rock and spotted thousands of people outside their new homes. The dew lifted from the ground and Sam noticed small, round cakes, almost as light as frost, at his feet. At first, Sam thought someone had dropped a fluffy biscuit beside him, but he noticed more behind him.

Micah stood at a high place and called out a greeting. "We need not ask ourselves, as the children of Israel did, 'What is it?' " he said. "For we know God has provided it as bread. Take, eat, and see that it is filling and sweet, like wafers made with honey. As Moses said to them, 'This is the bread which the Lord has given you to eat.' "

"Manna," Sam whispered.

Micah moved in front of a huge rock, planting his feet firmly in the loose rocks in front of it. "And what shall we drink? Again, God Almighty himself has provided."

Sam gasped as Micah raised both arms. Gushes of water sprang from rocks everywhere in Petra. Sam jumped down from his perch, put his hands under the fresh, cool stream, and drank.

Vicki followed Colin outside as darkness fell on Wisconsin. With the news that Lenore and Anita were safe in their Bolingbrook hideout, Vicki felt better about helping Anita. Now the kids in Wisconsin were on another potentially dangerous mission.

Earlier in the day, Vicki had received a message from those who had moved to western Wisconsin. Everyone had typed a few paragraphs on a joint e-mail that Vicki printed and read aloud to the others. Charlie said Phoenix was enjoying the new place. It even had a stream nearby that the two liked to play in. Darrion was sad about the lack of computer equipment, but she hoped to upgrade things soon.

Vicki thought of her friends as she checked her radio and settled into the underbrush near the woods. Colin had said there was a chance no one would come tonight, but they would reevaluate the mission after midnight.

In the stillness of the night, with crickets and frogs singing around her, Vicki's thoughts turned to Judd. Judd's recent phone call renewed her hopes that they would someday find a way to be together.

Vicki thought about the boys she had known in school. Most of them had been what her father had called "a bad influence," but that had simply made her want to date them more. Looking back, Vicki wished she hadn't gotten so involved in dating.

Vicki had once gone to a wedding of a distant cousin whose parents were into church. The couple had decided not to date but "court" each other. When she heard about the guidelines they had both lived by during their engagement, it had seemed strange and almost laughable.

"This is about the time first contact was made a couple of nights ago," Colin whispered into his radio. "I want radio silence and no movement."

Vicki leaned against a tree, closed her eyes, and smiled. She imagined sitting across from Judd in a parlor wearing clothes from pioneer days. "Judd comes a-courtin'," Vicki whispered. Was this all simply a dream, a fantasy she was creating? Or did God have a plan for the two of them?

Vicki had memorized two verses from Psalm 37 when she had lived in Pastor Bruce Barnes' home. As she struggled with her place in the world, he had suggested she learn Psalm 37:3-4. "Trust in the Lord and do good. Then you will live safely in the land and prosper. Take delight in the Lord, and he will give you your heart's desires."

At first, Vicki thought this meant that she had to forget about her own desires and concentrate on what God wanted for her. But Bruce had explained a different way to look at it.

"God gives each of us natural desires and abilities," Bruce had said. "In your heart, there are things you'd like to do, not sinful things, but things you're naturally drawn to."

"You mean, like helping younger people?" Vicki said. "I've always been good at baby-sitting and taking care of kids."

"Yes, if you like to do that, maybe God will one day give you children," Bruce said. "Or maybe he'll use you in another way to teach others. Some people think that to serve God, you have to do something you don't want to do. Sometimes that may be true. But other times he uses what's in your heart, desires for good things to bring him glory."

A twig snapped and brought Vicki back to reality. She glanced in Colin's direction but couldn't see him in the darkness. Conrad, Shelly, and Mark were also well hidden.

Vicki peered ahead, straining to see through the brush. Suddenly, a figure darted out of the blackness and rushed past her, only a few feet away. Vicki followed the figure with her eyes and noticed the long, black hair.

Colin clicked the radio twice, the signal for action. Vicki sprang to her left and grabbed the black-haired person by the ankles.

"Help!" came the high-pitched wail. It was the voice of a girl. "Daddy, help me!"

# TEN

# Tanya

VICKI held on tightly to the girl's ankles as the others arrived. The girl thrashed and struggled to get free when Colin turned her over and shined a flashlight in her face. There was no mark on her forehead.

"It's okay," Colin said quietly, trying to calm her. "We don't want to hurt you. We want to help you."

The girl's eyes darted to each face. She gasped when their radios crackled and Becky Dial asked for an update.

"Mission accomplished," Colin said. "We're headed your way."

Vicki helped the girl to her feet and asked her name.

"I'm not supposed to tell you anything," the girl said as they walked toward the house. "Are you Global Community?"

Vicki shook her head. "We're just as scared of the GC as you are."

Colin shot Vicki a look. "We'll talk more when we get inside. But we have to know, is there anybody else out there? Anybody looking for you?"

"No," the girl said, but Vicki wasn't sure she was telling the truth.

They took her inside the house where Becky had coffee brewing. The girl refused it and anything else to drink when Colin offered, and they sat at the table. The girl was a little over five feet tall, with jet-black hair that hung down in clumps. She wore a dark, leather jacket and black jeans. Everything was dark about her except her skin, which was quite pale. She had a thin, cute face and brown eyes. Vicki couldn't help thinking the girl looked like she could use a good meal.

As they talked, Vicki noticed a peculiar smell. The girl's clothes had an odor of damp, wet earth, much like the smell of Ginny and Bo's cellar back at their farm.

Colin and Becky moved to the corner of the kitchen, talking in hushed tones. A timer on the oven dinged, and Colin brought a plateful of biscuits and jam to the table. He turned a chair around and straddled it. "We don't mean to hurt you. What we said in the message we put on the tree was true. We want to help you, but you have to trust us."

Everyone took a biscuit. The girl watched them closely and finally grabbed one and ate it quickly.

"Whoa," Mark chuckled, "slow down." He got the girl a glass of milk, and she drank it in one gulp and reached for another biscuit.

Colin introduced everyone by first name only, and the girl glanced at each face through her stringy hair. When he had said everyone's name he turned back to her. "Now it's your turn."

She put down the biscuit she was holding and pulled a hank of hair back from one eye. "My name's Tanya. I think that's all I'd better tell you."

Colin nodded. "Okay, then let us tell you what we know about you. A couple nights ago, Vicki saw your face at one of our cameras. You've obviously watched our house long enough to know we have sensors out there to see intruders. You left a message that said you wanted help. But you're not alone. You called for your father when we caught you. Is he out there?"

The girl's eyes widened. "Don't bring my dad into this. He'll be really mad."

"Why?" Colin said.

"Because he doesn't understand. He thinks we can stay out here until this is all over, but I can't take it anymore."

Vicki touched the girl's hand. "You can't take what?"

"Being out there . . . where we live." She took another bite of biscuit and dropped her head. "I shouldn't be telling you any of this. He'll be really mad."

Vicki leaned over to Colin and whispered, "Maybe if I talk with her alone?"

Colin asked everyone to leave. When she and Tanya were alone, Vicki pulled a chair close. "We really do want to help you. You don't have anything to be afraid of."

"Then why did you guys jump me?"

Vicki bit her lip. "I guess we're just as scared as you are. We didn't know who you were. We still don't."

"Why are you guys hiding?" Tanya said.

Vicki knew she was talking with someone who wasn't a believer, but there was something innocent about Tanya that made her want to open up. "We think Nicolae Carpathia is an evil leader. And that no one should take his mark."

"What mark?"

"In order to buy or sell anything, people are being given a mark on their forehead or their right hand."

"The dragon," Tanya whispered. "This Carpathia dude is the head dragon of Revelation."

"You read the Bible?"

"My dad does. He believes the prophecies are coming true. That's why we went underground. The terrorists, or the dragon, were taking over, and it wouldn't be until Armageddon that we could come out again."

Vicki scratched her head. "So your dad believes in the Bible, but you don't?"

"Oh, I believe. It's just that I can't stay where we are anymore. It's too hard, too closed-in."

Vicki felt confused. If Tanya and her father were believers, why didn't she have God's mark? Vicki decided to get as much information as she could. "How long have you been living out there?"

"Since the war," Tanya said tentatively. "People disappeared. Then the GC started bombing and it was clear our Mountain Militia didn't have a chance, so we went underground like my dad had planned."

"Mountain Militia?" Vicki said. "MM."

"Yeah, we sewed that on our clothes because Dad told us to."

"How many of you are there?"

"There's my dad, my brother, and me.

Then there are the other families that followed us. Twenty-two people in all." Tanya closed her eyes. "My dad would kill me if he knew I was telling you this."

"Where do you stay?"

"It's partly a cave, I guess. My dad and some other men dug it out a long time ago without anybody knowing. They worked on it for a couple of years before the disappearances. My dad had the code worked out from his study of the numbers in the Bible."

"What do you do in the hiding place?"

"Exist basically. Most of us sleep during the day and stay up at night. I finally bugged Dad long enough that he started letting us go outside for some fresh air after dark. One night I walked over here and noticed the lights in the house. I came back a lot. I finally saw the cameras you guys have, and that's when I decided to ask for help. I wanted to see what you'd do."

"So the other night when I came outside?"

"That dog of yours just about scared me to death. My brother must have followed me because he caught the thing and tied it to a tree branch. I asked him not to tell anybody. He made me promise I wouldn't come over here anymore, but I couldn't stay away. I read the note you guys put out, and it made me think you might help me."

"Why did you cover the cameras?" Vicki said.

"I wanted to get closer to your place," Tanya said. "Maybe find some supplies. We're running low."

"What do you eat?"

"My dad stored canned and dry goods in there a long time before we moved in. We'll need to come out for supplies pretty soon."

"You won't be able to get any without the mark," Vicki said. "You've been living underground almost three years?"

Tanya raised her eyebrows. "It's murder on my tan, but I guess it's worth it since we're safe."

"The earthquake didn't affect you?" Vicki said.

"Sure did. One of our walls collapsed on a family. They're still buried in there."

"How awful."

"Yeah, and those stinging things—the ones that looked like little horses?"

"The locusts?" Vicki said.

"Whatever. They stung a couple of our people, but we plugged up the holes to keep them out. Our people didn't die, but they wished they could."

It was clear to Vicki that the people in Tanya's underground hideout weren't believers. "What did your dad do before the disappearances?"

"He owned a shop that sold guns, ammunition, old military equipment, and stuff like that. A lot of it was shipped via the Internet. He wrote a couple of books about what he believed was going to happen. That's how we met the different families who are staying with us. They all followed my dad and believed him when he said the holocaust was coming.

"When Chicago got hit, we went underground because of the possibility of radiation and everything. I guess it hasn't been as bad as we thought."

"Have you kept up with what's been happening around the world?" Vicki said.

Tanya frowned. "I haven't watched TV in three years. A couple of times my dad brought the radio out, but he says the media's all controlled by the GC, so he listens and tells us what he thinks is important."

Vicki thought of all that had happened in the past three and a half years. Tanya and her friends had remained safe, but they had missed so much. They also hadn't heard the truth about God.

"When you asked for help," Vicki said, "what did you want?"

"I guess I wanted out. I can't tell my dad

that, but I'm so tired of the same old food and the same stink under the earth. We're cold down there, it's hard to breathe, and there are snakes. It's not a nice place."

"I can't imagine spending three years underground."

Tanya's hair had fallen forward and she pulled it back again. "You don't know what I'd give just to take a shower. You must feel safe above ground. Why?"

For the first time since she had met the girl, Vicki felt an opening to tell her the truth about God.

As he waited for word from Westin, Judd tried to busy himself with the Young Tribulation Force's Web site, theunderground-online.com. More young people weighed in from around the globe about Carpathia's defeat in the desert and the safety God was providing in Petra. There were a few people who complained about "religious crazies" who wouldn't take the mark, but most of the comments and questions seemed sincere.

Chang Wong called from New Babylon and reported that more people were being given lie detector tests about the "mole" in the palace. "Since the big guy is back in town, everybody's testy. They've suspended tours of his new office."

"Did the construction affect your bugs?" Judd said.

"No. David Hassid thought of everything. They've made Nic's office bigger by swallowing up other offices. The place is absolutely huge. Plus, they put in a transparent ceiling so the king of the world can look straight into heaven if he wants. But I can still hear everything."

"What happened in the meeting of the world leaders?"

"I'm on my way home to listen," Chang said. "You want me to send you the file after I hear it?"

"Can you do that?" Judd said.

"Sure. I'll send you an encryption device to install on the computer you're using. And check out what's going on in Petra. They should have their computers up and running by now."

Judd hung up and called Lionel into the room. They found updates from Petra and a word-for-word account of Micah's message to those assembled in the area. News about the miracles of water flowing from rocks and wafers found in the morning dew was broadcast via the Internet.

Judd was thrilled when he read reports

from people who had passed the news on to others. Secret house churches were being formed around the world as people finally believed the truth about God's plan. An international revival had begun, and Judd wondered how long Carpathia and his troops would allow it to continue. Surely the pressure would mount on believers to toe the line, take the mark, and follow.

Judd couldn't wait to hear what Nicolae had said to the other world leaders.

Vicki scooted to the edge of her seat. "What do you think about God?"

"I don't know," Tanya said. "I don't really think that much about him these days. Everything seems like it's determined ahead. Who lives, who dies. What do you think?"

"Just like I think there's an evil person in the world, I believe God is working out a plan for good to those who believe in him."

Tanya rolled her eyes. "You call what's happening in the world good? From what my dad tells me, there's been a lot of people losing their lives. Now the oceans have turned to blood. Doesn't sound like God's doing a very good job."

"In the Bible, God said he would send his

Son to set the captives free. God's doing that right now for millions of people around the world. He did it for me, and he can do it for you too."

"You mean set me free from that hole in the ground?"

Vicki smiled. "Set you free from the bad stuff you've done. Set you free from fearing what the Global Community can do to you. God wants to make you his child, to become part of his forever family."

"Dad says only 144,000 are going to be saved, and he wants us to be part of that. Are you saying he's wrong?"

"I don't know enough about what your father believes," Vicki said, "but I do know that the Bible says anyone who believes in Jesus and trusts in him alone will be saved."

"Jesus was a great prophet," Tanya said. "I believe he lived a good life and showed us—"

The door to downstairs burst open, and Vicki heard the faint sound of an alarm in the background. Mark and Colin stood in the kitchen, looking out the back window.

"What's wrong?" Vicki said.

"Sensors went off," Colin said. "Somebody's headed this way."

# ELEVEN

# Carpathia's Scheme

VICKI jumped up and turned off the lights.

Tanya pushed her chair back and joined them at the back window. "This could be my dad or my brother," she said. "Let me go outside—"

"Just stay here," Colin said.

"There!" Mark pointed. "Behind that tree. I saw movement."

Before Colin could stop her, Tanya ran outside, slamming the door behind her. Vicki strained to see out the window. In the moonlight, Tanya raised her hands. "Ty? Dad? It's me. Don't shoot."

A muffled shout came from the trees. "They're good people," Tanya replied. "They don't want to hurt us."

Finally, a young man who looked a couple of years older than Tanya walked forward carrying a shotgun at his side. Tanya opened the door.

Colin stepped in the doorway. "I need you to leave your gun outside."

"Come on, Ty," Tanya said, "it's okay."

Ty put his gun by the door and followed Tanya inside. Colin held out a hand and introduced himself. Ty looked away.

"These people are okay," Tanya said.

"Dad told you about making contact. Let's go." Ty grabbed Tanya's arm and pulled her toward the door.

"Wait," Vicki said. "We have supplies. I know you're running low. . . ."

Ty glared at his sister. "How much did you tell them?"

"Please listen," Tanya said. "There's something different here."

"If you don't come with me now, I'm telling Dad, and you know what he'll do."

Tanya's eyes widened and Vicki sensed real fear. "I'll be right out," she said.

Ty nodded. "I'll wait outside."

When he was through the door, Tanya turned to Vicki and the others. "I don't understand everything you said, but I know you've got something I don't have."

"God loves you enough to die for you."

"But if I believe what you say, I'll be going against my dad."

"Don't believe what I say," Vicki said. "Read it for yourself." Vicki grabbed a Bible and opened it.

"I don't have time right now," Tanya said.

Vicki bit her lip. "Stay with us. We can show you the truth. . . ."

Ty pecked on the window and motioned for Tanya. She turned back to Vicki and shook her head. "I have to go. For your sakes and mine. If Dad found out . . ."

She put a hand on Vicki's shoulder. "Maybe I'll be back."

Tanya slipped into the night. Vicki prayed she would have another chance to talk with the girl.

Judd told Lionel what Chang had said, and soon he had the encryption file installed on the computer in Westin's hotel room. Westin returned as Judd downloaded the file containing Carpathia's meeting with his potentates.

"You should erase that as soon as you've listened to it," Westin said. "I don't want Z-Van or anybody else finding it and knowing we have access to that stuff."

"Did Z-Van say anything about getting out of here?" Lionel said.

"He said he wouldn't talk about leaving until the plane arrives. He's basking in the world attention right now. They're trying to get his new CD out as quickly as they can. People are eating it up."

Chang had written a brief note attached to the file. *Here's Nicolae in his glory. I'd tell you to enjoy the recording, but after hearing what's on it, there's no way. I wish I could send this to my mother to show her how evil the man is, but I don't dare risk my father seeing it. He might turn me in.*

Judd punched up the recording and heard Carpathia waste no time blaming the blood-in-the-oceans disaster on God's people. Judd tried to imagine Nicolae in his new office, the gleaming, glass ceiling above him.

"Who have been among the last to embrace Carpathianism?" Carpathia railed. "The Jews. Who is their new Moses? A man who calls himself Micah but whom we believe to be none other than the Jew who vainly assassinated me, Dr. Chaim Rosenzweig.

"Who are the Judah-ites? They claim to be Jesus-followers, but they follow Ben-Judah, a Jew. Jesus himself was a Jew. They are fond of referring to me as Antichrist. Well, I will embrace Anti-Jew. And so will you. This is war, gentlemen, and I want it waged in all ten regions of the world."

"Uh-oh," Lionel said. "Here comes the plan."

Carpathia explained that he intended to wipe out all Jews and Judah-ites around the world and that he would start with Petra as soon as Tsion Ben-Judah arrived to speak there.

"They are now all in one location, and as soon as Ben-Judah makes good on his promise, we will welcome him with a surprise. Or two. Or three. Security and Intelligence Director Suhail Akbar . . ."

"Thank you, Your Worship," Akbar said. "We are carefully monitoring the activities of the Judah-ites, and while we have not infiltrated the Jews at Petra, they have confined themselves to that area, saving us the work. We are prepared to rally two fighter-bombers when we know Ben-Judah is en route—we believe him to be only one or two hours from Petra anyway—and we should be able to drop one annihilation device from each craft directly onto Petra, literally within minutes of his arrival. We will follow with the launch of a missile that will ensure total destruction. That was scheduled to be launched from an oceangoing vessel but will now be launched from land."

Judd shuddered at the thought of bombs

being dropped on Petra. The people wouldn't have a chance unless God somehow intervened.

Carpathia picked up the plan and continued. "The Judah-ites have proven to be such hero worshipers and so dependent on the daily Internet babblings of Ben-Judah that his death alone may mean the end of that nuisance. While we are aware of other pockets and strongholds of Judah-iteism, we do not believe any other leader has the charisma or leadership required to withstand our unlimited resources.

"But make no mistake, my loyal friends. The Jew is everywhere. Is there one potentate here who would aver that you do not have a significant Jewish population somewhere in your region? No one, of course. Here is the good news, something to make you forget the inconvenience of this journey I required on short notice. I am opening the treasury for this project, and no reasonable request will be denied. This is a war I will win at all costs.

"Maintain your loyalty mark application sites and make use of the enforcement facilitators. But, effective immediately, do not execute Jews discovered without the mark. I want them imprisoned and suffering. Use existing facilities now but build new centers as soon as possible. They need not be fancy or have any amenities. Just make them secure. Be creative, and share with each other your ideas. Ideally, these people should either long to change their minds or long to die. Do not allow that luxury.

"They will find few remaining Judah-ites to sympathize with them. They will be alone and as lonely as they have ever been, even though their cell mates will be fellow Jews. There are no limits on the degradation I am asking, requiring, you to inflict. No clothes, no heat, no cooling, no medicine. Just enough food to keep them alive for another day of suffering.

"I want reports, gentlemen. Pictures, accounts, descriptions, recordings. These people will wish they had opted for the guillotine. We will televise your best, most inventive ideas. From time immemorial these dogs have claimed the title to 'God's chosen people.' Well, they have met their god now. I have chosen them, all right. And they will not find even death a place they can hide.

"Apply for all the funds, equipment, rolling stock, and weapons you need to ferret out these weasels. The potentate who demonstrates the ability to keep them alive the longest, despite their torment, will be awarded a double portion in next year's budget."

Judd stopped the recording and looked at

Lionel and Westin. "Tsion Ben-Judah said Carpathia would attack God's people."

Lionel grabbed a Bible and flipped to Revelation. "I was reading something interesting this morning. In Revelation it talks about the dragon chasing a woman, who I think is Israel. Listen to this. 'Then the dragon became angry at the woman, and he declared war against the rest of her children—all who keep God's commandments and confess that they belong to Jesus.'"

"Carpathia is the dragon about to make war on all Jews and all believers," Westin said.

Judd punched the play button again, and Carpathia's voice filled the speakers. Nicolae told the group that he no longer needed sleep or food and that he wanted video recordings of executions. Moments later, Carpathia announced that the group would witness the death of two stewards accused of supplying information to outsiders. Judd knew this was false, that Nicolae would kill these two simply for the sport of it, and it turned Judd's stomach.

Vicki hated to see Tanya leave, but she knew they had to let her go with her brother. Everyone in the house went downstairs and prayed for her and asked God to open her heart to the truth. Conrad prayed, "Father, we don't just ask for Tanya and her brother, but for everyone in that place to hear about you."

When they finished, Colin asked, "What did Tanya tell you about her dad?"

Vicki told him. "It sounds like he's into some weird theology. From what she said, her dad uses the Bible like some kind of code-book. He has them all believing everything's going to be okay as soon as the final battle ends."

"He's right about there being a final battle," Mark said, "but if he doesn't believe the truth about God, everything's not going to be all right for him and the people with him."

Though she was exhausted, Vicki found it difficult to sleep. She tossed and turned in bed, then finally fell asleep and dreamed that Tanya's father came for them in the night with a machine gun.

The next morning everyone met for breakfast and prayed again for Tanya and the people with her. Conrad reported that there had been no activity outside after Tanya and Ty had left.

"You did a wonderful thing reaching out to that girl," Becky said to Vicki.

"I should have done more. I could have

given her something to read." Vicki ran a hand through her hair. "I can't help thinking that her dad will punish her for coming to see us. Maybe try to brainwash her against the truth. She's cut off from everything."

"We have to trust God to help her," Colin said.

Sam sat with Naomi Tiberius and marveled at the complex computer system set up in Petra. It felt like such an odd mix of primitive living conditions and modern technology. Only a few yards from these state-of-the-art computers, people slept in tents and ate food and water provided miraculously by God. Inside the building, where the computers were protected from the heat and dirt, Naomi monitored Chang's transmissions and the news from New Babylon, and helped train volunteers to send information via computer to anyone who e-mailed them.

"How long until Dr. Ben-Judah gets here?" Sam said as Naomi pulled up a report from GCNN.

"He's still in the States. No word on his arrival time yet. We have a message from Chang that something's brewing inside the Global Community."

"Another attack?"

"I'm not sure, but we'll need to let Micah and the other leaders know. From what Chang says, the GC is decimated."

A GCNN report tried to put a pretty face on the water problem. Engineers worked around the clock, but they couldn't figure out how the blood problem began or what to do to stop it. Footage from a helicopter showed rotting sea creatures floating on one ocean's surface. Medical authorities warned that disease could bring about the most serious health crisis in history.

Sam sighed. "I know a bigger crisis to people's souls, but they won't report that."

# TWELVE

# Warning Angel

JUDD felt frustrated about Z-Van's airplane. When it was delivered, Westin went to inspect it. Judd and Lionel continued monitoring the latest news along with the kids' Web site. Curious e-mails had been sent from around the world about citizens angry at Nicolae Carpathia.

*This is even coming from people who have already taken Carpathia's mark*, one person from Australia wrote. *They are upset about what happened in Israel, and they don't see any progress in clearing the waters of blood.*

"You can bet the GC will have something to say about that," Lionel said.

Lionel was right. A news bulletin flashed over the Global Community News Network. "At noon today, Palace Time," a news anchor said, "Carpathianism's Most High Reverend Father, Leon Fortunato, will deliver a live message to the entire world. This broadcast will be repeated every hour for twenty-four hours so everyone around the world will see or hear it."

Judd quickly wrote a message for theunderground-online.com and said everyone should pay attention to Fortunato's announcement. The kids would follow Leon with their own commentary.

As the official GC announcer appeared onscreen, Judd clicked the record button so he could copy the text of Leon's message word for word. "We go live now to the sanctuary of the beautiful Church of Carpathia off the palace court here in New Babylon and the Reverend Fortunato."

A massive choir, dressed in their finest robes, stood behind Fortunato as he stepped into the pulpit. Leon looked even stranger than usual, now wearing a flat-topped hat. His outfit seemed to try to incorporate sacred symbols from every religion.

"He looks like a clown trying to get into a church." Lionel smirked.

The choir struck up a solemn version of "Hail Carpathia," as Leon raised his head in worship. Finally, he spread his notes before him and looked into the camera.

"Fellow citizens of the Global Community and parishioners of the worldwide church of our risen lord, His Excellency, Supreme Potentate Nicolae Carpathia . . . I come to you this hour under the authority of our object of worship and with power imbued directly from him to bring to you a sacred proclamation.

"The time has expired on any grace period related to every citizen receiving and displaying the mark of loyalty to Nicolae Carpathia. Loyalty mark application centers remain open twenty-four hours a day for anyone who for any reason has not had the opportunity to get this accomplished. Effective immediately, anyone seen without the mark will be taken directly to a center for application or the alternative, the enforcement facilitator."

Lionel gave Judd a worried look. "We should have gotten out of here a long time ago."

"Furthermore," Leon continued, "all citizens are required to worship the image of Carpathia three times a day, as outlined by your regional potentate, also under threat of capital punishment for failing to do so.

"I know you share my love for and dedication to our deity and will enthusiastically participate in every opportunity to bring him praise. Thank you for your cooperation and attention, and may Lord Nicolae Carpathia bless you and bless the Global Community."

Judd turned back to his computer, but

Lionel pointed to the TV screen. The lights had gone out in the church, and a murmur rose from the assembled crowd. When the lights came back on, the choir were stumbling over themselves, some motioning toward the ceiling and reacting in horror.

The picture shook and wobbled but remained on. A video crawl asked viewers to stay tuned. Judd turned up the volume and heard frightened worshipers stampeding toward the doors. Suddenly, a glowing face appeared on-screen and lit Westin's hotel room. The voice boomed over the speakers and Judd grabbed the remote. Even though he turned the volume down, the voice could still be heard in the room.

"If anyone worships the beast and his image," the voice said, "and receives his mark on his forehead or on his hand, he himself shall also drink of the wine of the wrath of God, which is poured out full strength into the cup of his indignation. He shall be tormented with fire and brimstone in the presence of the holy angels and in the presence of the Lamb.

"And the smoke of their torment ascends forever and ever; and they have no rest day or night, who worship the beast and his image, and whoever receives the mark of his name.

"Here is the patience of the saints; here are

those who keep the commandments of God and the faith of Jesus.

"Blessed are the dead who die in the Lord."

Vicki had awakened the moment she heard the voice. She ran to the main room of the hideout and found Shelly watching the monitors and a special GCNN report.

"I was going to wake you guys," Shelly said, "but they said they were going to re-air Leon's announcement every hour, so I decided to let you sleep."

A GCNN anchor tried to compose herself as she stared into the camera. "We apologize for that malfunction, which should be ignored. We will now show Reverend Fortunato's message in its entirety again."

Leon appeared on the screen. "Fellow citizens of the Global Community . . ." But Leon's voice and face were blocked out as a bright light shone on-screen and a heavenly face overwhelmed it. The angel repeated the message that no one should worship the beast or take his mark on their forehead or hand.

The GCNN anchor returned and squinted at a TelePrompTer under the camera. "Because of a technical difficulty the network will be off the air until further notice." The screen went black, but the angel appeared again. No matter what the Global Community technicians tried to do, they couldn't stop the shining face or the loud announcement.

As soon as the face had appeared on their computer screens in Petra, Sam Goldberg ran outside and looked into the sky. The sun was high above, beating down, but the face of the angel appeared even brighter. The image was overpowering, and the people perched along the rocks of Petra fell to their knees.

Sam had often heard people talk about God and ask why he didn't speak from heaven and tell people who he was. Now this heavenly being was warning people around the world about Nicolae. Tears sprang to Sam's eyes. An overwhelming sense of peace flooded his soul. Though it seemed, at times, that evil would cover the whole world, God was truly in control.

Sam wondered how anyone could question Carpathia's true identity or God's love.

Judd noticed an e-mail from Chang and quickly opened it. He thought it would be

more bad news from Carpathia, but he was
surprised to find Chang excited about the
angel's message and a note about Chang's
family.

> *I wrote my mother and told her briefly of*
> *Carpathia's next plans. They are going to*
> *torture Jewish people instead of giving them*
> *the guillotine. They say the blade is too*
> *good for them.*
>
> *My mother just wrote the following to me:*
> *"Your father says we will risk our lives,*
> *live in hiding, or face the death machines*
> *before we will take the mark. He is nearly*
> *suicidal over forcing you. I tell him you*
> *already sealed by God, and so is Ming. I*
> *will connect to Ben-Judah Web site. We*
> *will be worshipers of God and fugitives.*
> *Pray."*

Vicki spent the next day watching the monitors for any sign of Tanya and her brother.
She prayed that the voice of the angel had
penetrated the deep recesses of the cave
where they were living.

Her hopes diminished as the day wore on.
Shelly joined her at one of the computers,
and the two spent an hour uploading mate-

rial to people who had written about the angel's message.

*If we take the mark of Carpathia, God will kill us, and if we don't take the mark of Carpathia, the Global Community will kill us,* one man wrote from Sri Lanka.

*Better to obey the One who has the power over the soul than those who can simply kill the body,* Vicki wrote back.

Lionel packed the few things he had and prepared to leave Israel as soon as Westin gave the word. The problem was, Westin hadn't called, and Lionel was worried Z-Van might have turned him into the GC authorities.

The phone rang and Lionel picked up, only to hear a recorded message from the front desk to tune their television to the hotel's channel. He and Judd saw a recorded message by the hotel manager.

"In compliance with the Global Community's latest directive, we are urging all guests who have not yet taken the mark of loyalty to our lord and king, Potentate Carpathia, to do so immediately at the nearby loyalty mark application site."

A map of the area flashed on the screen with a red *X* near the hotel. "You may exit the hotel, turn left, and go two blocks to receive the mark. The procedure takes only a few minutes, and since it is now required on penalty of death, the hotel will no longer accept guests who do not have the loyalty mark.

"We will soon be making a room-to-room sweep, along with Global Community personnel, so we urge you strongly to make your way to the application site within the hour."

Lionel heard movement in the hallway and checked the peephole. Several people hurried to the elevator. A door across the hall opened, and a man and woman rushed into the hallway, still slipping on their shoes.

"I wonder if it's like this all over the world," Lionel said.

"I heard that this hotel is owned by a rabid Carpathia follower," Judd said. "The room is under Z-Van's name, so I think we'll be okay as long as we can hide."

"Where's Westin?" Lionel said.

Judd shook his head. "Good question. We'd better unhook the computer and get ready to leave."

A buzz ran through Petra as Sam headed to check in with Naomi at the computer center. Several top leaders hurried from the building. Sam found Naomi, who told him Tsion Ben-Judah was on his way by helicopter.

"Don't look too excited," Naomi said.

"How can I not be excited?" Sam said. "The person who has meant most in my life other than Jesus himself is coming to speak to us."

Naomi stared at him. "Chang just e-mailed us and said he overheard a conversation between Carpathia and one of his directors. Nicolae wants Petra leveled within minutes after Dr. Ben-Judah's arrival."

"An attack?"

"Fighter planes will drop bombs, and then a missile will be launched from Jordan."

Sam felt like he had been punched in the stomach. After seeing the earth swallow the Global Community army, he had believed God would protect them. Now a fear so real he could taste it crept over him.

"How much time do we have?" Sam said.

Naomi turned toward the door as two Israelis rushed inside. "The helicopter is coming!" the man shouted. "Dr. Ben-Judah is almost here!"

Vicki sat alone at the monitors. She had volunteered to take the late-night watch for a reason. Now, a few minutes shy of 4 A.M. and with her relief two hours away, Vicki grabbed the plastic bag she had filled with materials, flipped off the motion alarms, and slipped quietly outside.

She had thought of arguing with Colin, Mark, and the others about her plan, but she was convinced they would never agree. Maybe this was something she would regret, something she would have to apologize for, but she knew she had to take the chance.

The truth was, Vicki felt responsible for Tanya. She had tried to tell her the message of life, but Tanya had been whisked into the night. The thought nagged at Vicki every time she looked at the monitor and saw the silent forest staring back at her.

*If I can find their cave, or even get close enough to it to leave these printouts from our Web site*, Vicki thought, *I'll leave them and get back to the hideout before anyone knows.*

She passed the tree line they had stared at for the past few days and walked into the dense woods. A hundred yards farther she turned on a flashlight and realized she was near a gully. A few more steps and she would have fallen over the edge.

Vicki was going on the vague sense of direction Tanya had given her from their conversation in the kitchen. Vicki figured she might see footprints or a path of some kind.

She glanced at her watch. It felt like she had been outside at least an hour, but it was only a few minutes. She panned the nearby hillside with her flashlight and switched it off. Nothing. She turned back the way she had come and panicked. She didn't recognize anything. She was less than half a mile from Colin's home, but she had made so many twists and turns that she was now lost.

A twig cracked nearby and Vicki stopped. She tried desperately to still her breathing. Someone was out there. Should she call out or wait? If it wasn't Tanya or her brother, would she be shot?

Vicki crouched low and prayed.

Sam took his place among the crowd inside Petra. He estimated there were at least 200,000 inside and probably three or four times that outside, waving at the helicopter and cheering.

Micah was just above Sam on a high place overlooking the city. The large, flat spot had been prepared for the landing, and Sam covered his eyes as the chopper's blades kicked up dust. Tsion Ben-Judah stepped out of the helicopter and waved at the people as Micah greeted him with a hug.

When the helicopter's engine shut down, people cheered again, and Micah raised a hand. "Dr. Tsion Ben-Judah, our teacher and mentor and man of God!"

Tears filled Sam's eyes as he looked toward the man who had led so many to the truth about Jesus Christ. When the crowd quieted, Tsion said, "My dear brothers and sisters in Christ, our Messiah and Savior and Lord. Allow me to first fulfill a promise made to friends and scatter here the ashes of a martyr for the faith."

Dr. Ben-Judah removed the lid from a small container and shook the contents into the wind. "She defeated him by the blood of the Lamb and by her testimony, for she did not love her life but laid it down for him."

Sam turned his head to avoid getting some of the ashes in his eyes and noticed something in the distance. Above the desert came two specks.

Fighter planes!

People pointed and murmured as the two jets screamed toward Petra.

Dr. Ben-Judah got the attention of the crowd and held out his hands. "Do not be distracted, beloved, for we rest in the sure promises of the God of Abraham, Isaac, and Jacob that we have been delivered to this place of refuge that cannot be penetrated by the enemy of his Son."

The planes passed overhead with a roar and banked in the distance. Sam thought that perhaps God would knock them from the sky or envelop them in fire, but they continued. Tsion paused until the noise died. The planes turned and headed back toward Petra.

"Please join me on your knees," Tsion said, "heads bowed, hearts in tune with God, secure in his promise that the kingdom and dominion, and the greatness of the kingdom under the whole heaven, shall be given to the people of the saints of the Most High, whose kingdom is an everlasting kingdom, and all dominions shall serve and obey him."

Sam closed his eyes and knelt with a million other people. As the jets neared Petra again, he wondered how God could possibly keep them safe.

# ABOUT THE AUTHORS

**Jerry B. Jenkins** (www.jerryjenkins.com) is the writer of the Left Behind series. He owns the Jerry B. Jenkins Christian Writers Guild, an organization dedicated to mentoring aspiring authors. Former vice president for publishing for the Moody Bible Institute of Chicago, he also served many years as editor of *Moody* magazine and is now Moody's writer-at-large.

His writing has appeared in publications as varied as *Reader's Digest, Parade, Guideposts*, in-flight magazines, and dozens of other periodicals. Jenkins's biographies include books with Billy Graham, Hank Aaron, Bill Gaither, Luis Palau, Walter Payton, Orel Hershiser, and Nolan Ryan, among many others. His books appear regularly on the *New York Times, USA Today, Wall Street Journal,* and *Publishers Weekly* best-seller lists.

Jerry is also the writer of the nationally syndicated sports story comic strip *Gil Thorp*, distributed to newspapers across the United States by Tribune Media Services.

Jerry and his wife, Dianna, live in Colorado and have three grown sons.

Dr. Tim LaHaye (www.timlahaye.com), who conceived the idea of fictionalizing an account of the Rapture and the Tribulation, is a noted author, minister, and nationally recognized speaker on Bible prophecy. He is the founder of both Tim LaHaye Ministries and The PreTrib Research Center. He also recently cofounded the Tim LaHaye School of Prophecy at Liberty University. Presently Dr. LaHaye speaks at many of the major Bible prophecy conferences in the U.S. and Canada, where his current prophecy books are very popular.

Dr. LaHaye holds a doctor of ministry degree from Western Theological Seminary and a doctor of literature degree from Liberty University. For twenty-five years he pastored one of the nation's outstanding churches in San Diego, which grew to three locations. It was during that time that he founded two accredited Christian high schools, a Christian school system of ten schools, and Christian Heritage College.

Dr. LaHaye has written over forty books that have been published in more than thirty languages. He has written books on a wide variety of subjects, such as family life, temperaments, and Bible prophecy. His current fiction works, the Left Behind series, written with Jerry B. Jenkins, continue to appear on the bestseller lists of the Christian Booksellers Association, *Publishers Weekly*, *Wall Street Journal*, *USA Today*, and the *New York Times*.

He is the father of four grown children and grandfather of nine. Snow skiing, waterskiing, motorcycling, golfing, vacationing with family, and jogging are among his leisure activities.